FALKIRK COMMUNITY TRUST

D.A.

CANCELLED

30124 03060688 5

Falkirk
**Community
Trust**

Bo'ness
01506 778520

Bonnybridge
01324 503295

Denny
01324 504242

Falkirk
01324 503605

Grangemouth
01324 504690

Larbert
01324 503590

Meadowbank
01324 503870

Slamannan
01324 851373

This book is due
for return on or
before the last date
indicated on the
label. Renewals
may be obtained
on application.

Falkirk Community Trust is a charity registered in Scotland, No: SC042403

2 8 FEB 2017

1 3 SEP 20
28 SEP 20

2 3 OCT 201

- 3 JAN 201

1 0 MAR 2018

1 4 JUL 20

0 7 JAN 2019

2 1 MAR 2019

2 1 JUN 2021

1 5 DEC 2023

KU-750-410

Brothers of the Gun

Buford Lance fought for every inch of his B-L connected ranch, so he'd be damned if he was going to hand over a large portion of his Cottonwood Creek range to homesteaders.

Instead, he decides to fight again. This time, he hires two of the best guns in the business.

Lucas Kane: The Gun King. They said he was invincible, that there was nobody faster.

Jordan Kane: The Prince. Next in line for the throne. He'd take on any job. It was said that he'd shoot his own mother if the price was right.

One, an out and out killer, the other, his polar opposite who could never commit murder, no matter the price. When Lucas Kane refuses the job, Lance has him bushwhacked.

It begins an infamous blood-letting talked about for years to come and leads to the change of a town's name in an effort to forget.

Ultimately, it draws two brothers into a showdown where only one can walk away.

Will the 'Gun King' keep his throne? Or can the 'Prince' finally get to wear the crown he desperately covets?

By the same author

Fury at Bent Fork
Brolin

Brothers of the Gun

B.S. Dunn

A Black Horse Western

ROBERT HALE

© B.S. Dunn 2017
First published in Great Britain 2017

ISBN 978-0-7198-2125-7

The Crowood Press
The Stable Block
Crowood Lane
Ramsbury
Marlborough
Wiltshire SN8 2HR

www.bhwesterns.com

Robert Hale is an imprint
of The Crowood Press

The right of B.S. Dunn to be identified as
author of this work has been asserted by him
in accordance with the Copyright, Designs and
Patents Act 1988

Falkirk Council	
Askews & Holts	2017
AF	£14.50

Derek Doyle & Associates, Shaw Heath
Printed and bound in Great Britain by
CPI Group (UK) Ltd, Croydon, CR0 4YY

This one is for Sam and Jacob.

PROLOGUE

Cottonwood Creek Range: Present Day

Thirty years, the lone man marvelled. Had so much time passed since it had happened?

He sat on his horse at the top of a tree-lined hill and looked out over the farms along Cottonwood Creek.

He was in his mid-sixties; his hair grey and his face cut by lines of age and hard work.

He could remember the emptiness when there was nothing here but Cottonwood Creek itself and mile upon mile of grazing land.

Then the settlers had come, hauling with them a world of hurt that saw the range run red with blood.

The old man shook his head as he remembered the killing. So many innocents had died because of one man's greed.

Somewhere in the distance, a whip cracked, loud enough to reach his ears. It sounded like a gunshot and he instantly dropped his hand to his thigh and went for a gun that was long gone.

'Old habits,' he grunted to himself.

He dropped his gaze to a large stand of cottonwoods. A graveyard, now home to many of the original homesteaders who'd fought for what was theirs because they had nothing else, lay deep within the circle of trees.

There was a noise beside him and a woman of about thirty-six, with long flowing black hair, halted her bay mare beside him.

'It's certainly changed from what it used to be, hasn't it?' she commented.

The man nodded. 'Yeah, it sure has.'

He paused then asked, 'What brings you up here?'

'You do,' she answered. 'I know you come up here every year at this time. What's it been? Thirty years now?'

'Yeah, thirty years.'

The time had passed quickly and it seemed just like yesterday that hell had come to the Cottonwood Creek range.

CHAPTER 1

Before

Buford Lance sat quietly atop a flat, copper-coloured rock and surveyed his kingdom, everything before him as far as the eye could see. The late afternoon sun had already begun its slow but steady descent towards the mountains.

He was a tall man of fifty-five years, with grey hair and brooding grey eyes. His face was lined from years of hard toil and his scuffed range clothes bore similar signs to those of his features. From his position on the sparsely covered ridge, he could see the thousands of acres he claimed as his own; hard-won acres.

On first arrival at the foot of the Sangre de Cristo range, with a few head of cattle and a head full of dreams, he'd faced many trials. They'd included every two-legged outlaw around these parts, plus Arapaho Indians, Kiowa and Southern Cheyenne.

Thankfully, he was still alive to tell the tale and had himself the biggest ranch around. Lance even had the honour of having the town named after him.

Buford had become a thriving town which supported the surrounding ranches and homesteads. It was also used as a supply point for prospectors who travelled deep into the Sangre de Cristo Range.

His kingdom was some of the best grazing land around. It was crisscrossed with streams lined with cottonwoods. There were great stands of aspen, fir and spruce trees. The great bald, rocky crags and snow-capped peaks of the Sangre de Cristo Range provided a stunning backdrop to all this beauty. Magnificent giants that thrust their hands from the wilderness in an attempt to touch the sky.

He paused and thought once more of the homesteads. They were the bane of his existence. They'd come into his territory and tried to take this land that he'd fought so hard for. Armed with their papers and their so-called rights to 160 acres. At first, he'd allowed a few to settle, but the floodgate had never closed and a torrent had washed into his valley. They were not the ones who'd fought for this land. They'd not shed a drop of blood for it. What gave them the right? Certainly no piece of paper.

His bay horse snorted an alarm and brought Lance back to the present. He looked down to the base of the slope and saw a rider approach at a fast gallop. When the man's horse hit the incline, he spurred it on, urging it to climb faster.

When horse and rider reached the top, he rapidly dismounted and strode across to the bench where the old rancher sat.

'We got problems, Buford,' gasped Chuck Lane. 'Big problems. I just came from town and the hands said you were up here.'

Lance studied his foreman's square-jawed face and saw concern etched deep in his brown eyes.

'Take your time and tell it to me straight, Chuck,' Lance said measuredly.

Chuck removed his brown Stetson and slapped at the dust on his blue jeans and shirt. He ran a calloused hand through his hair and took a deep breath to compose himself.

Chuck had been foreman of Lance's B-L connected spread for the past ten years. He'd worked for him much longer, but now at forty, he was Lance's most trusted and relied on man.

'I went to town this mornin' to get some supplies 'cause Chowhound was runnin' short of things to try and poison us with,' he started to explain. 'While I was in the store, I overheard some of them homesteaders, talkin' about more of 'em comin' to Buford to take up homesteadin'. So after I finished loadin' up the wagon I went and seen that lawyer feller, Grimsby.'

'What did he have to say?' Lance asked in his customary gravelly voice.

'He said it was true,' Chuck nodded. 'Only this time it's not just one or two takin' up their quarter section. This time, there is a whole wagon train of 'em comin' in to set up on the range by Cottonwood Creek. The lot of it.'

Lance turned and looked toward his land to the south. 'How many, Chuck?'

'Accordin' to Grimsby there's twenty families comin' in.'

Lance's face contorted with rage at the prospect of having so much more taken from him. Twenty quarter sections; just over 3,000 acres of prime grazing land. Not to mention good water for his cattle and some large tracts of timber.

'No, God damn it!' his voice rumbled. 'No damn sodbuster is comin' in here and takin' all of that range from me. I fought for it and I aim to keep it.'

Lance stood and began to walk towards his bay. 'Come on, Chuck.'

'Where are we goin'?'

'Back to the house,' Lance answered. 'There's only one way to stop what's comin' and that's with guns. I'm not givin' them one inch of my graze. The government says they have to be there five years to make the land theirs. They ain't goin' to be there five damned minutes.'

'Here,' Lance said as he held out a piece of paper. 'Take this to Grimes and tell him to find these men.

12

I don't care how many wires he has to send or what it costs. Just tell him I want 'em all found.'

Chuck read the paper by the dull lamplight in the ranch house living room, looked at his boss then read it one more time.

'Are you sure about this, boss?' he asked cautiously.

'Yes, damn it. I've never been surer about anythin' in my life before. I want those men. It's the only way to stop them sodbusters from stealin' my range.'

Chuck folded the paper and tucked it into the top pocket of his shirt. 'Fine, if it's the only way, then me and the boys will back you one hundred per cent.'

Lance nodded. 'Thanks, Chuck, I knew I could count on you.'

A whole town held its collective breath as Lucas Kane, the 'Gun King', faced down three Shaw brothers in the dusty main street of Spanish Fork, New Mexico. Jeb, Seth, and Mo stood shoulder to shoulder, totally undaunted by the man who stood before them.

Lucas Kane was thirty-four and his solid 6-foot-1 frame cast a long shadow in the afternoon sun. His hair was black and his brown eyes stared hard at the brothers while his right hand rested on the butt of his holstered Colt Peacemaker which was tied down low.

His blue pants and buckskin jacket were well worn but in good repair.

The Shaw brothers were well known, tenth-rate

13

back shooters who'd ridden into Spanish Fork a month before. The first day in town, they'd taken out the local sheriff and since then, had waged a campaign of fear and violence.

Jeb and Seth were the older brothers, both in their thirties, thin and unkempt. While Jeb was of average height, Seth was tall at 6-foot-4. Both wore Colt .45s and knew how to use them.

Mo was cut from a different bolt of cloth. At twenty-eight, he was fat and well groomed. He tried to keep himself as tidy as possible, but as an outlaw found it nigh on impossible. Like his brothers, he wore a Colt .45 but instead of a Stetson, he preferred a derby style hat. Unlike his brothers, his nervousness showed openly in these situations.

Mo would be the last shot. Kane's assessment of the three was that Mo would shoot too quick and miss, which would give him more time.

He was certain he could take the other two, even on his worst day.

'Are you ready to die, Kane?' Jeb Shaw snarled from his position twenty paces away. 'Even you ain't that good. You're outgunned, so there's no way you can beat all three of us.'

'Just waitin' for you to start the ball,' Kane replied, 'then we'll see if what you say is true.'

Jeb Shaw licked his lips and shot a glance over Kane's right shoulder then settled his gaze once more on the gunfighter.

Kane frowned. It was the second time he'd looked that way.

Crowds lined the boardwalks on both sides of the street as they waited patiently, onlookers at some bizarre sideshow.

'You boys can still walk away,' Kane informed them. 'Just turn around, get your broncs and leave town.'

'The hell we are,' Seth cursed. 'We ain't goin' nowhere. But you are, Kane, feet first into the ground.'

They were Seth Shaw's final words. He grabbed at the butt of his holstered Colt and started his draw.

The six-gun was still pointed down when the first slug from Kane's Peacemaker blew through his teeth and out the back of his head. The impact sprayed splinters of skull and grey brain matter onto the street behind him.

Kane moved his aim slightly and fired again, this time at Jeb Shaw. The bullet slammed into Shaw's chest before he could clear leather. His mouth flew wide as he gasped with pain and Kane fired again. The second slug hit the outlaw in the throat and bright red blood sprayed over Mo.

Shock registered on the younger brother's face when he realized that he too would suffer the same violent fate as his brothers.

Kane had been wrong about him. Mo had been so scared that his fear had rendered him incapable of even attempting to draw his gun. The youngster froze then cried out, 'No, wait!'

The gunfighter pulled his finger back from the trigger of his Peacemaker then realized that Mo hadn't shouted at him. The younger brother's gaze was directed behind Kane. He whirled about desperately, looking for the back shooter he knew must be there.

Once more, a gunshot thundered and the sound reverberated around the false fronts of the buildings on the main street. Kane spotted the bushwhacker and snapped the Peacemaker into line with his target. He was too late; the man had already buckled at the knees and slumped to the ground. A red stain spread across his shirt.

Kane looked about the crowd of onlookers, in search of the person responsible for the shot. Out into the street stepped a tall figure, dressed in jeans, red shirt, knee high boots and black Stetson. His left hand held a still smoking six-gun.

'Thought you were more careful than that, Lucas,' the newcomer observed.

Kane was about to say something when a voice suddenly screamed, 'Lookout!'

Kane spun around to find Mo Shaw bringing his gun into line. His courage had grown remarkably when Kane's back had been turned. Two shots rang out and the younger Shaw died beside his brothers in the dust of Spanish Fork's main street.

The newcomer walked forward and stopped beside Kane. 'I see you're startin' to slip a little, Lucas.'

'Yeah, Rio,' Kane allowed as he ejected the empty cartridges from his Colt and thumbed in fresh loads. 'I must be gettin' old. Thanks for your help, by the way.'

Rio Smith was a man made from the same mould as Lucas Kane. A hired gun with a reputation for taking only the honest jobs.

'Mr Kane?' an uncertain voice wavered from behind the two men.

They turned and Kane recognized the mayor of Spanish Fork. In his hand he held an envelope which the gunfighter assumed contained his payment.

The portly man stepped forward. 'There you are, Mr Kane, one thousand dollars, just as you asked.'

Kane took the money and nodded. 'Thank you, Mayor.'

The civic leader smiled timidly then turned and hurried off.

'What are you doin' in town, Rio?' Kane asked as he stuffed the money inside his shirt.

'Just passin' through,' Rio explained. 'Been down in old Mex helpin' out some villagers who had trouble with a local bandit. Turned out he was American. An outlaw by the name of Bob Flint.'

Kane nodded. 'Come on, let's get out of the street. I'll buy you a drink. I guess it's the least I can do since you saved me from a bullet in the back.'

17

'Where are you headed?' Kane asked as he placed the empty shot glass on the scarred tabletop.

Rio looked about the brightly lit room. The Hashknife saloon was almost full. Tables were jammed with customers as they excitedly related their version of what they'd witnessed in the street.

'I'm headed north. What about you? Anythin' on?'

'Nope, might head over to Texas, see if anyone is hirin' ranch hands.'

Rio looked as if he'd been slapped in the face.

'What?' said Kane.

'Did I hear you right?' Rio managed to get out. 'You did just say "ranch hand".'

Kane shrugged. 'What can I say? I like cows.'

Rio shook his head in disbelief.

A short, wiry man with hair parted down the middle entered the saloon and Kane watched his progress as he made his way through the crowd to the long, timber bar. He saw the man speak to the elderly barkeep in the large mirror which hung on the wall behind the counter. The barkeep pointed to Kane and the man turned and walked towards the table where the two gunfighters sat.

The man stopped in front of them and asked nervously, 'Mr Kane?'

Kane nodded. 'What can I do for you?'

The anxious man smiled faintly. 'My name is Bentley, Cyrus Bentley. I'm the telegraphist here in town.'

18

Bentley held out a folded piece of paper for the gunfighter. 'This came for you earlier.'

Kane took the paper, thanked the man and tipped him four bits for his trouble.

Bentley smiled thinly, thanked Kane then hurried off through the crowd.

The gunfighter read the note then placed it in his pocket.

'Work or trouble?' Rio asked.

'Work,' Kane confirmed. 'A place called Buford, up in the Sangre de Cristo foothills. Must be important, feller is offerin' a thousand.'

'Sounds like a real earner,' Rio acknowledged. 'Just be careful, Lucas, as you know high payin' jobs usually come with high risk.'

'Ain't that the truth. Feel like some company on your way north?'

'Sure, why not? Be glad to have you along.'

CHAPTER 2

Jordan Kane felt a buzz course through him and he smiled. Today he was going to kill a man. Not because he needed killing, but because he could. Payment for the job made it feel just that much better.

He looked at his reflection in the fly-specked mirror and liked what he saw. A tall, lean but muscular body clad in black clothes, black Stetson with a silver band and black leather gun rig with silver conchos. The holsters housed a matching pair of nickel plated, ivory handled Colt .45s.

He relaxed briefly then drew his six-guns, a smooth, fluid draw that was almost invisible to the eye.

Jordan smiled at himself and his reflection smiled back.

He was a young man at twenty-six, and the Prince was what they called him. The King in waiting. He was sure that it wouldn't be much longer before he would be at the top, and his brother could walk in his shadow. If Lucas was still alive.

He knew the day would come when he faced his brother over blazing six-guns. He would win of course, of that he was sure.

For now, he had a job to complete. He was in the town of Berry, Colorado, population 876, soon to be 875. He'd been hired by a local rancher having trouble with smaller homesteads refusing to sell. The sheriff was sticking his nose in where it wasn't wanted so Jordan was hired to cut that nose off.

There was a knock and Jordan turned to face the door. 'Yeah what?'

The door swung open and a diminutive man stood on the threshold. He instantly cowered at the sight of two Colts pointed in his direction.

'Don't shoot me!' he cried out.

Jordan smiled coldly and holstered his six-guns. 'Don't go frettin' none, little man, if I was goin' to shoot you, you would already be dead. Now, what do you want?'

'My name is T . . . Teague, I have a t . . . telegram for you,' the man stammered.

Jordan motioned to an old, scarred side table against the far wall. 'Put it over there and get out.'

Teague's hand trembled as he placed the folded piece of paper on the dark table top. He turned back to the killer and waited expectantly.

'Is there somethin' else you want?'

'Well . . . um normally . . . when I. . . .' He stopped again.

'Oh, you want a tip. A little somethin' for your trouble, is that it?'

A nervous smile accompanied a slight nod.

Jordan drew his right side Colt and aimed at Teague.

The telegraphist paled noticeably and screeched, 'No wait! Don't!'

Teague turned and stumbled from the room; the harsh laughter of Jordan Kane followed him along the hotel's hallway.

The killer kicked the door shut and walked across to the table. He scooped up the note and read the scrawl through twice just to make sure he understood the content.

He was to go to a town called Buford then out to a ranch called the B-L connected. It seemed the owner was willing to pay him a thousand dollars to solve a problem.

He decided that he would pay the rancher a visit, but if the man wanted his services, they would cost him more than a thousand dollars. After all, if you need the best, you pay for it. Now for the other matter.

Frank Alexander cursed himself for letting things get this far out of hand. He knew from experience that quicker action should have been taken and now he had to go up against a cold-blooded killer with an almost insurmountable reputation.

He walked across his office to the gun cabinet and took out a sawed-off Greener. He opened a box of shells loaded with double-ought buckshot and stuffed two of the shells into the twin barrels. He snapped it closed and cursed himself again.

'You're a damned old fool.'

Alexander had been a sheriff for thirty years, and at fifty-five had slowed down some and made the decision to give it away soon. As he picked up his sweat-stained Stetson and jammed it down on his grey hair, he thought that maybe yesterday would have been the perfect day to do just that.

He hitched his pants around his bulging middle and took one last look around the jail. After this was over, he thought that he might get one of the town ladies to come in and do a little cleaning for him. Yeah, maybe he'd ask widow Jones or Jenny the mayor's daughter to do it for him.

As Alexander closed the door, somewhere deep inside him knew that it was the last time.

He didn't have far to go to find the man he was looking for. As luck would have it, Jordan Kane was coming down the street.

The townsfolk of Berry knew something was imminent as whispers had begun circulation upon the

Prince's arrival in town. On the deeply rutted main street, in full view of the town's citizens, some on the boardwalks, others tucked away inside the many false-front stores, the time for that something to happen had arrived.

Alexander swung the scattergun up and thumbed back both hammers.

'Hold it right there Kane!' he called loudly.

Jordan stopped, twenty feet from the sheriff. He dropped his gaze to the gaping barrels, then back at the man pointing them. 'Can I do somethin' for you, sheriff?'

His aged face set hard, Alexander nodded. 'You can get the hell out of Berry and not come back. That's what you can do for me, killer.'

Hands on the ivory handles of his guns, Jordan shook his head. 'Now that ain't right friendly, sheriff, tryin' to run a feller out of town on what – his third day here. And having done nothing wrong.'

'I don't care. We don't want your type here. So you can saddle up and ride.'

Jordan's face remained passive and he shook his head again. 'Nope, can't.'

Alexander's right eye began to twitch nervously. 'Can't or won't?'

'I've a job to do, sheriff. Already been paid so I guess this is it.'

'What?'

Jordan smiled mirthlessly. 'I guess this is where we

24

find out if I can beat the drop of them hammers on that scattergun you're holdin' on me.'

Alexander's eyes grew wide in disbelief and uncertainty. It was the distraction Jordan needed and he drew. People swore later that they didn't see what happened. One instant the Prince was standing there relaxed and the next, his hands were full of six-guns, bellowing out their throaty roar.

Both bullets hit Alexander dead centre, no more than two fingers' width apart. The lawman was dead before he realized it. The unfired shotgun fell from lifeless hands and clattered to the hard-packed earth. Alexander's legs gave out and he slumped to the ground beside the gun.

Jordan twirled his six-guns in a display of arrogance and flipped them back into their holsters. He smiled and boasted, 'Damn, I'm good.'

A heavy downpour had passed over Buford just prior to Lucas Kane's arrival and his buckskin mare splashed through the mud and brown water puddles in the main street. His slicker was still damp and he looked forward to getting dry.

Townsfolk stared, curious as to whether the stranger would stop in town or pass right through. A buckboard rumbled past with a load of supplies accompanied by a couple of cowhands on their way out of town.

It was shortly before noon so Kane decided to

stable the mare, have something to eat, then later in the day, ride out to the B-L connected ranch and meet the owner.

Further along the street, he found what he wanted. Nestled amongst the false-front stores and other businesses was a livery where he could leave the mare.

After seeing to his horse, he found a hotel for the night and changed into some dry clothes. There was a small cafe two doors from the Cattleman's Bank, beside a boarding house and Kane decided to get a feed.

The sign above the door said, 'Lisa's kitchen, travellers welcome'. Kane pushed the door open and entered. Square tables sat in neat rows. They were adorned simply with white cloths and clean cutlery.

The establishment looked clean and well patronized and a few lunch clientele sat around, finishing their meals, several of whom looked up, the rest paid him no mind. Kane found an empty table and sat down.

He hadn't been seated long before a slim young lady, with long black hair and a pleasant smile emerged from the kitchen to take his order of steak, fried potatoes, gravy, and coffee. She apologized that there was no dessert but explained that it was an evening thing and if he wanted apple pie, he'd have to come back at supper time. He smiled and watched her walk off.

Next, the town sheriff arrived and sat on the chair opposite Kane at the table. He was a man of about middle age, average build, and height, with dark hair and grey eyes.

'Can I help you, sheriff?' he enquired.

'Well Kane, that depends on you,' the man explained. 'My name is Thomas Brooks and as you can see I'm the sheriff of Buford.'

'Do I know you?' Kane asked.

'No,' Brooks allowed, 'but I know you. I've seen you in action and I know your type. Your kind attracts trouble where ever you go.'

'So what is it you want from me?' Kane asked patiently.

'Honestly? I want you gone from my town. Stay the night if you must but be gone by mornin'.'

'Well that's mighty generous of you, sheriff,' Kane said evenly. 'But you see, I happen to be here about a job out at the B-L connected. So at this time, I'm goin' nowhere.'

Kane let Brooks digest the information and could see the man's mind tick over.

'Damn ornery son of a bitch,' he burst out, 'I knew there was goin' to be trouble when that old buzzard found out.'

Kane was puzzled. 'How's that?'

Brooks lurched up from his seat. 'You'll find out. I just hope that when it all happens, you're on the right side of the law.'

Kane remained silent and watched the lawman leave.

When Kane stopped on the low hill, he saw the B-L connected ranch headquarters up ahead on a flat rise a mile distant. It was set amongst tall trees to the rear and sides, and the front had a steep embankment of some thirty feet in height. It was a prime position to sit and look out over their range.

At the base of the embankment, a shallow stream followed the contour then disappeared into a stand of cottonwoods.

Kane kneed his buckskin forward off the hill and out on to the large flat tract of grazing land, where numerous cattle fed lazily on sweet grass. At the stream, the trail dipped through the water and out the other side. It curved away to the left and followed a cut up through the embankment until it levelled out at the top.

From there, it went straight on for thirty yards until a grandiose arch over a large gate allowed access into the main ranch yard. Kane rode through the gate and looked around as he crossed to the house.

The set-up was impressive. The main ranch house was a magnificent double-storey timber affair with white walls, mullioned windows and a large veranda that wrapped around the whole building. The second-storey veranda only covered the front of the house. It had a hand-tooled balustrade painted white, and two sets of French doors that opened from the front bedrooms. There were three stone chimneys and a peaked slate roof.

To Kane's left stood a large timber-planked barn and bunk house. In the shade of a large pine and set back right of the bunkhouse, was a corral with a couple of horses. Long stables stood off to the right with a water trough out front and a hand pump on one end.

Kane noticed the horse tethered at the hitch rail near the trough. It was a big black stallion, with a silver concho-studded Mexican saddle on his back. Kane knew immediately whose horse it was as he'd seen it before. He cursed under his breath and turned the buckskin toward the other mount.

He dismounted and tied it to the rail. He glanced once more at the black then turned to walk across to the house, but found someone blocking his way.

'Can I help you stranger?' Chuck asked.

'I'm here to see your boss. The name is Lucas Kane.'

The foreman nodded. 'Follow me.'

The inside of the ranch house appeared to be as grand as the outside. It reminded him of pictures he'd seen of plantation houses from the deep south. Through the large double hardwood doors was a staircase, wide at the base and tapered all the way to the top. The reception room floors were marble, freighted in especially for the project.

The rooms were luxuriously appointed and everywhere that Kane looked, it was evident that masses of money had been spent on every fixture, fitting, painting, and rug.

'Follow me, Kane,' Chuck said.

They walked along the hall to the third door where the foreman knocked, then entered. Kane followed him in. The room was well lit with natural light from a large mullion window. The floor was covered in carpet and throughout the room was a scattering of hand-made furniture. A grey-haired man who was seated in a brown leather-backed chair rose to greet him.

'At last,' he said warmly. 'You made it. I'm Buford Lance.'

The cattleman stepped forward with his right hand extended. Kane hesitated before he took it in his firm grip. 'Pleased to meet you, Mr Lance.'

Lance could read the puzzled expression on the gunfighter's face and said, 'Yes, Kane, the town is named after me. I came here when it was just wilderness and now they're tryin' to take it away from me.'

'I see,' Kane said seriously.

'Damn homesteaders, Kane,' Lance explained. He gestured towards a man who leaned against a red cedar mantle over an open fireplace. 'I believe you two know each other.'

Kane turned to see the mirthless smile of the man standing there holding a glass of whiskey. Still the same Jordy, he thought. Same clothes, same fancy gun rig.

'What are you doin' here, Jordy?' he asked in a hollow voice, devoid of emotion.

'Hell Luke, is that any way to greet your long-lost brother?' Jordan asked, his voice laced with sarcasm.

'I couldn't care less if I never saw you again, Jordy. Plain and simple,' Kane informed his brother.

Jordan clenched his hands and his eyes narrowed. 'Damn you, Lucas, still playin' at bein' the king. No time for anyone else but you.'

Kane ignored the comment and turned to face the rancher. 'What's he doin' here, Lance?'

'He's here because he's one of the best,' Lance answered, 'just like you. And for this job, I need the best. You see, there is a wagon train of homesteaders coming here to put down roots on some of my best range. Land that I fought for over many years.'

'What about the Homestead Act, Lance?' Kane asked. 'Do you have title to that range or is it free graze? Because if it's free graze, there's nothin' to say they can't homestead it.'

The rancher's eyes blazed. 'It's what I say, damn it. They'll not turn one sod, put up one damn home on that land. They are not wanted here and you two are goin' to make that happen.'

'What about the ones who are already here? I saw

31

at least one on my ride out here.'

'They go too,' Lance explained. 'I've been too soft on them so I want them run off as well.'

'And the law? I met the sheriff in town. What about him?'

Lance set his jaw firm. 'If he gets in the way he'll have to be dealt with. Do you have a problem with that?'

'I don't,' Jordan assured Lance.

Kane stared at the rancher for a long time before Jordan broke the uneasy silence. 'What about money, Lance? How much are you payin'?'

'One thousand, like it said in the telegram.'

Jordan shook his head. 'Nope. If you want me to kill the sheriff, you're goin' to have to come up with more than that. Besides, I wouldn't even get out of bed for that amount.'

'Fine,' Lance snapped. 'How much?'

'Five thousand.'

The rancher's face remained passive as he considered the amount, then he said, 'Done. Both of you will get five thousand upon completion of the job. Satisfied?'

Jordan smiled and took a sip of whiskey from the glass he held.

'No.'

They both looked at Kane.

'What?' snapped the rancher, who showed obvious distaste at the answer he'd been given. 'What do you mean, no?'

Kane stared into the man's eyes and refused to be intimidated. 'Exactly how it sounds.'

Jordan laughed loudly. 'Hell, Lance, I almost forgot. You see my brother has a conscience. Imagine that, a killer with a conscience.'

'Is that true?' Lance asked.

'If not wantin' to commit murder for the likes of you means that, then yeah, it's true,' replied Kane evenly. 'And the other problem I have is that I don't work with killers. That's exactly what my brother is. A stone cold killer.'

'Wow, brother,' Jordan sneered, 'that's mighty rich comin' from a man who's killed more than me.'

Kane rested his hand on the butt of his Peacemaker. 'At least I can say that every man who died by my gun was facin' me, little brother. Can you say that?'

A dark cloud of rage settled on the younger Kane's face. Through gritted teeth he said, 'Better watch your mouth, Lucas.'

Without taking his eyes from his brother, Kane spoke clearly. 'I'm leavin' now, Lance. You can keep your money. But if you want my advice, forget what you're about to do. No good can come of it. And most of all, don't hire my brother. If you do, you're just askin' for trouble.'

Without another word, Kane backed out of the room and closed the door.

The furious rancher swung his head to look at Jordan. 'Well, are you stayin' or goin'?'

'I'm stayin'.' A cold smile spread across the killer's face. 'Unlike my brother, I don't much care who I have to kill.'

'Good, get squared away then I'll fill you in on what I want done.'

'Sure.'

Lance watched Jordan Kane leave then waited a few minutes before he called his foreman into the room. 'Bring in the other one.'

Several minutes later a new man entered the room. He wore jeans, a blue shirt, leather boots and a grey Stetson. A tied-down holster on his right hip housed a Colt Army model. Adorned on the holster was a single concho.

Concho Bell was another gunfighter in the elite league. He was six feet tall and was as slim as a rail.

'Are you ready to start earnin' your money, Concho?' the old rancher asked.

Concho Bell nodded. 'Just tell me what you want done.'

'I want you to kill Lucas Kane,' Lance announced. 'Can you do it?'

'Yeah I can do it,' answered Concho, 'but not straight up. I'm not goin' to take that chance. He's not called the Gun King for nothing.'

Lance nodded. 'Come over here.'

The rancher crossed the room and stood in front

34

of a large map which hung on the wall. 'See this here? This is where we are. This here,' he continued, 'is the main trail into town. Now if you ride this way through here. . . .'

A thorny finger traced a path from the ranch to a point where the trail horseshoed. 'Tucked in here is a big outcrop of rock. A great place to wait.'

'He's got a good start on me,' Concho pointed out.

'Not if you take the cut-off like I just showed you. You'll beat him there and have time up your sleeve. Once you are done,' Lance pointed at another spot on the map, 'hole up here. There's a line shack you can use. If I need you I'll send a man. If not it will be the easiest five thousand you'll ever make.'

'Well then, I'd best be movin'.'

'One more thing, Bell, don't miss. He knows too much.'

Concho Bell didn't even blink when he boasted, 'I don't miss.'

CHAPTER 3

Lucas Kane felt obliged to inform Brooks of the storm that was about to rain down upon his territory and urged his horse along at a canter. He'd warn him then leave town. He wanted to put as much ground between himself and his brother as possible.

There was no love lost between the two of them. Jordan had taken to the gun trail five years ago at the age of twenty-one. When Lucas Kane had begun to make a name for himself as a famous gunfighter, the stories began to filter through to home and Jordan had left then to try to do the same.

At first, Kane's brother had taken to testing his speed on easy marks. Cowhands and drifters were his early prey. Then, in the small town of Porter in Kansas, Jordan came across a gunfighter named Jim Kent. A man of some repute, Kent was said to have killed five men in stand-up fights.

Kane's understanding of the way it went down was

that, as soon as Jordan had discovered the identity of the man, he'd braced him in the saloon and kept pushing until there was no other option left open to Kent but gun play.

When the gun smoke had cleared, the gunfighter lay dead on the sawdust-covered planks with two holes in his chest, his gun still in his holster. Men swore they didn't even see Jordan draw.

From that moment on, he'd been chasing the title his brother held. Not caring how he achieved it, he wanted to be the best and Kane knew that one day Jordan would call his hand. It was for this reason that he had to leave. When all was said and done, Jordan was still his brother.

A giant mass of boulders loomed in the distance where the trail horseshoed around them. Great grey slabs piled atop one another stood out like a beacon across the land. Kane kept the buckskin at an even pace; scattered pines flitted by as he rode on.

As he rounded the bend, Kane moved the horse to the outside of the trail, away from the deep rut that had worn over time. He caught a blur of movement high in the rocks, but by then it was too late.

A rifle whip-lashed and Kane felt the blow of the bullet as it buried into his side. He was hurled from the saddle and landed heavily on the hard-packed trail, which knocked the air from his lungs. His head connected solidly with a protruding rock and bright lights flashed in front of his eyes before his whole world went dark.

Up amongst the rocks, a lone figure stood, his eyes on the prone form below, ready to fire his Winchester at the first sign of movement. He waited for a brief time and when Kane didn't move, he turned away, sure his job was done.

If Concho Bell had waited a little longer, he would have seen Kane move his arm.

As Kane rolled on to his back, pain from the bullet wound in his side ripped through him and caused him to moan. He could hear voices far off in the distance, incoherent murmurings that he couldn't understand. His eyes flickered open and the sun's harsh glare almost blinded him.

Again the voices came to Kane. Distant. Incoherent. He opened his eyes once more and a kaleidoscope of faces swirled in front of him. Pain drummed through his head, his eyes closed and again blackness claimed him.

When Kane next opened his eyes, it was dark. He was in a soft bed with clean blankets over him and his wound had been bandaged. Pale moonlight shone through a side window which provided limited illumination in the room.

Kane tried to move but the pain in his side ripped through his body and took his breath away. He could feel the bandages wrapped around his lower torso.

He lay there and tried to piece together the events which had led to this point. The more he thought about it, the job, the ambush, all that remained were questions.

'Hello?' Kane called out.

It was more a croak than anything.

He cleared his throat. 'Hello?'

As he waited, Kane heard soft footfalls on a timber floor. The door to the room opened and a woman dressed in a nightgown entered the room with a kerosene lamp.

Instinctively, Kane pulled the bed covers higher in her presence.

'You're awake,' she said. Her voice had a soft lilt.

'Where am I?' Kane asked.

'That's not important at the moment,' she said softly. 'Get some more rest and we'll talk in the morning.'

'What's your name, ma'am?' he asked.

'It's Martha Hamilton,' she replied. 'My husband, Brock, found you on the trail. Now, no more questions.'

Kane watched Martha leave the room with the lamp which left the bedroom in darkness once again.

He closed his eyes and went back to sleep.

In the morning, Kane was already awake when Martha Hamilton returned.

In the light of day, he could make out the features

of the soft-spoken woman.

He guessed her age to be around thirty-one and she was slim with a grey gingham dress which hung loosely on her delicate frame.

Martha's brown eyes were the same colour as her long hair which was tied in a bun. The flawlessness of her complexion struck him as odd due to the harsh conditions of living here in the west.

'Are you OK?' Martha asked.

'Ahh . . . yes ma'am,' Kane stammered. 'I'm sorry ma'am, I didn't mean to stare.'

Martha smiled warmly. 'Are you hungry?'

Kane nodded. He realized how hungry he was once food was mentioned.

'Yes, ma'am. I feel as though I could eat a horse.'

Martha laughed.

'I don't think horse is on the menu for breakfast,' she said. 'But I can find something for you, Mr. . . ?'

'Name's Kane, ma'am.'

She nodded. 'Mr Kane, I'll send my husband in and he can answer any questions you might have while I fix your breakfast.'

Martha hadn't been gone long when a small head poked around the corner of the doorway and said, 'Hello.'

Kane frowned. 'Hello.'

'Who are you?' a little girl with flowing black hair asked.

'I'm Lucas,' Kane answered. 'Who are you?'

'I'm Elsie,' she answered, then added proudly, 'I'm six.'

Kane was about to say something more when he heard Martha's voice call out to Elsie and the little girl disappeared.

When Brock Hamilton entered the room, Kane's first impression of the man was that he was exactly like his wife, warm and friendly.

Hamilton was a couple of years older than his wife. He was of similar stature and even shared the same coloured hair and eyes.

'Glad to see you awake, Mr Kane,' he said as he offered his hand. 'I'm Brock Hamilton.'

Kane took the calloused hand in a firm grip and shook it.

'Your wife tells me I have you to thank for finding and saving me.'

'It could have been anyone,' Hamilton said. 'I just happened to be comin' along the other day and found you. Couldn't leave you layin' there so I brought you back to our homestead.'

Kane frowned. 'The other day? How long have I been here?'

'This is the third day.'

Kane remained silent, deep in thought.

'My wife doctored you,' Hamilton explained. 'You see, she was a nurse in St Louis before we moved out here. She knows what she's doing, even took care of the fever and all.'

41

'Sounds like I have a lot to be thankful to you and your wife for.'

'Mr Kane, somethin's been buggin' me ever since I brought you here,' Hamilton said uncertainly. 'I'm not normally one to pry into another man's affairs but in this case, I think I must. Not for me but I have Martha to consider and we have a little girl called Elsie.'

Kane's face remained passive. 'I know, we just met.'

Hamilton frowned but let it go and continued. 'Our homestead borders Buford Lance's B-L con-nected and where I found you . . .' Hamilton's voice trailed away uncomfortably.

'The answer is yes,' Kane said in answer to the man's unfinished question. 'I was comin' from seein' Lance.'

'Are you a hired gun?'

Kane stared pointedly at Hamilton before he answered. But then, the man and his wife had taken him in.

'I am,' he said truthfully. 'But before you go jumpin' to any conclusions I turned down the job that was offered.'

'What was it he wanted you to do?'

'Nothin' more than plain murder.'

Hamilton thought for a brief moment then a look of recognition came across his face. 'Are you him? Are you that Kane?'

'Depends on which Kane you think I am.'

'What do you mean?' a soft voice asked.

Martha Hamilton stood in the doorway with a plate of food for Kane.

'I'd hold off on the breakfast, ma'am,' Kane told her. 'At least, until you hear what I have to say.'

'What? Why?'

'It so happens that I'm a gunfighter, ma'am,' he explained. 'My name is Lucas Kane.'

'Oh.'

Kane turned his attention to Hamilton. 'Is that who you thought I was?'

He shook his head. 'No. I thought you were the other one. But you bein' here is just as bad. When you've had your breakfast I'll ask you to leave.'

'Brock!' Martha protested. 'He's still not well enough.'

Kane nodded. 'It's OK, ma'am. I understand. Your husband is just lookin' out for his family.'

Her face grew stern. 'You'll leave when you are well enough and not a moment before.'

The last part was directed at her husband.

'OK, fine. But when he's well enough. . . .'

'I won't stay any longer than need be,' Kane confirmed.

Kane saw a brief hint of relief on Hamilton's face. 'Thank you.'

'I take it that before when you said the other one you meant Jordan?'

Hamilton nodded.

'He's here you know,' Kane confirmed. 'I'm pretty sure that it was him who shot me.'

Hamilton's face paled noticeably.

'Who's Jordan?' Martha Hamilton asked.

'He's my brother,' Kane said.

'And he shot you?' she asked incredulously.

'I believe so.'

'But why?'

Kane sighed. 'How about I start at the beginnin'.'

When he'd finished, Kane waited for their reaction. He could see their minds working.

'I'll get dressed and be gone,' Kane said to break the long silence.

'No!' Martha Hamilton said loudly. 'You need to rest.'

'She's right,' her husband said which totally surprised Kane. 'If you don't rest up your wound might open up again. Plus you've been out to it for a couple of days.'

'I need to tell the sheriff. . . .'

'I can do that,' Hamilton assured him.

Kane considered the offer and nodded. 'OK then. But be careful. Now how about that breakfast. I'm starved.'

'And you say he thinks his brother is the one who shot him?' Brooks asked, and raised his wild grey eyebrows.

'I think he's almost sure of it,' Hamilton confirmed. 'He said he was on his way here to warn you.'

Brooks climbed out of his battered office chair and walked across to the window. He looked out at the people on the street as they went about their business, totally oblivious to the storm which was about to envelop them and change their lives forever.

Brooks turned to Hamilton. 'I knew there would be trouble when he showed up. But with his brother here it is a whole different situation.'

'How so?'

'Jordan Kane will be here for me,' Brooks informed him. 'If I become a problem that is. I guess it goes to show just how serious Lance is about keeping the Cottonwood Creek range for himself.'

'What are you going to do?'

'Not much I can do at the minute,' Brooks informed him. 'Nothing has happened.'

'What about Kane being shot?'

'Tell him to come see me when he's up and about.'

Hamilton was puzzled. 'What for?'

'Just tell him to come see me.'

Three days later things changed, and they found out how serious the rancher was.

Lance scowled at the interruption and he looked up from the paperwork on the hardwood desk at the sound of the knock. The door swung open and Chuck entered the room with one of the ranch hands.

'What is it, Chuck?' Lance asked impatiently.

'Crandle here just rode in from the Cottonwood Creek range,' Chuck explained to his boss. 'He's been over there on watch.'

'And?' the rancher asked tersely.

'The homesteaders have arrived.'

Lance nodded slowly and looked at Crandle. 'Good work.'

Crandle stood there for a moment until a nudge from the foreman indicated that he was to leave the room.

Lance watched him go then said to Chuck, 'Get Kane and tell him to bring his hired men. It's time he earned his money.'

CHAPTER 4

A line of twenty canvas-covered wagons arrived with their weary owners on the Cottonwood Creek range. Drawn by four-horse teams, the heavy conveyances were laden with everything that the homesteaders owned.

The sun was not long past its zenith when they began to set up camp a short distance from the cool clear waters of Cottonwood Creek. It had been decided that they would disperse to their quarter sections tomorrow to begin their new lives.

Ernest Hughes stood outside the loosely circled wagons and stared in awe at the surrounding countryside.

Huge snow-capped mountains towered into the sky. Tree-clad ridges and foothills could supply their timber needs and the fertile ground and water from the creek would sustain their crops or whatever else they chose to do with it.

He watched an elk venture out of a stand of spruce on a far ridge and look the new arrivals over. Hughes smiled and said quietly, 'God has provided.'

He was a religious man in his first year past thirty. He was very tall and the past few weeks of travel had tanned his face several shades darker than it had been before.

'Sure is mighty fine country, Ernest,' a voice said, intruding on Hughes' reverie.

He glanced briefly at the man beside him then returned his gaze to the view. 'It sure is, Floyd, it sure is.'

Floyd Long was in his early forties and had been allocated the quarter section next to Hughes'. Though shorter than Hughes, there was a distinct difference between the neighbours. At Long's waist, there was a gunbelt with an old 1863 Remington converted from cap and ball to cartridge. Hughes never wore a gun.

They stood in companionable silence and continued to take in their new surrounds when nine riders appeared on a low hill to their north.

'Who do you suppose they are?' Floyd asked.

Hughes remained silent but eyed the men curiously as they sat there and watched them. Suddenly the group moved forward down the hill and approached the wagon train.

Initially, they bunched up but gradually spread out in a line as they neared the encampment. There was something menacing about it that made Hughes feel uneasy.

'I don't like this,' he said to Floyd.

Floyd's hand dropped to his six-gun.

'You ain't the only one,' he agreed.

When the riders drew closer, Hughes realized the cause of his unease. Every one of the riders wore a hood over his head.

'Oh my lord,' he heard Floyd gasp hoarsely.

'We need to warn the others,' Hughes said as he turned.

He ran back within the circle of wagons and shouted as loud as he could. The alarm had sounded throughout the immigrant camp and all of the new arrivals prepared to meet their attackers.

Floyd Long froze as he stared at the oncoming threat. He stood transfixed by the sight and sound, unable to react as the thunder of thirty-six hoofs echoed in his ears and the vision of so much horse-flesh bearing down upon him rooted him to the spot.

He was shocked quickly back to reality when the first shot came and whipped close by his head. He immediately went for the holstered Remington.

His momentary paralysis had caused too big a delay and before he could get the six-gun halfway clear, a bullet smashed into his chest and knocked him off his feet.

The riders thundered into the centre of the loosely circled wagons and drew up sharply. They fired at random targets as their horses milled.

Hughes dived under a wagon with his wife, Rose. He was in shock after being witness to Floyd's callous death. His hands now held a Winchester rifle. He worked the lever and jacked a round into the breech.

Before he could fire, he watched in horror as a homesteader by the name of Marsh fell to the ground with several bullets to the front and rear of his torso.

Hughes' wife's screams filled his ears at the sight of the dead man. He gritted his teeth and fired at one of the riders and watched the man slump forward in the saddle.

Another rider holstered his weapon and moved his horse in close to assist the wounded man.

A fusillade of shots peppered the wagon Hughes had taken refuge under and wooden splinters scythed through the air. He hugged the ground as more slugs carved into the wagon.

The mêlée continued. Cries of pain, horses screamed and attackers shouted. Though he couldn't see what they were doing next, Hughes had a fair idea that their stock was being slaughtered as well.

Cows, horses, and chickens they'd brought with them were targets.

Hughes could hear one man clearly shout orders. As he peered out, he could make him out amongst the phalanx of riders. The man was dressed completely in black; apart from the hood that he wore.

He saw the rider take deliberate aim at a home-steader trying to shield his young daughter. Without a second thought, Hughes fired the Winchester at him but missed badly. The shot lanced through the neck of the rider's horse, just below the mane. The sudden pain caused the horse to rear up and throw off the man's aim.

Hughes heard the killer curse loudly then shout orders to the other riders.

As quick as they had come, they were gone. They left in their wake a knot of crying women and children, as well as the wounded, dying and dead.

'Will it work?' Buford Lance asked as he sipped whiskey from a crystal tumbler and leaned back in his comfortable chair.

Jordan Kane shrugged. 'It may take more.'

'Well, we'll just hit 'em again,' Lance said with finality. 'And again and again, until they get the message or they are all dead. What about the men you hired?'

'They're at the old minin' shack you said to use,' Jordan told him. 'One of 'em was wounded but he'll be fine.'

Lance nodded. 'Good. I have another job for you and I want it done tonight.'

'OK.'

'I've come to the conclusion that I want all of the

homesteaders gone. Even the ones who are established.' Lance let his words sink in before he continued. 'I intend to buy or try to buy them out at my price. But before I make any offers to them I want them to understand the ramifications if they refuse.'

'So what is it that you want me to do?' Jordan asked.

Lance took another sip of whiskey, put the glass down and stood up. He crossed to the map on the wall.

'Let me show you. . . .'

Three bullets punched into Kane from the flaming barrel of the Colt Peacemaker. Every impact jarred his body and sent bolts of pain through him. He could taste the blood in his mouth as his lungs filled, every breath became shallower and shallower.

Kane felt the strength start to ebb from him and he sank to his knees. The six-gun became too heavy, fell from his grasp, and thudded into the dust of the street.

His vision began to blur and Kane could feel himself cant forward. He fought for breath but his lungs were almost full of blood and the air came in short sips.

The all-consuming blackness began to rush towards him and he felt himself fall forward and hit the ground.

With his dying breath he whispered, 'Why, Jordy?'

Kane came awake with a start. He'd had this particular dream before and knew that he would again.

He looked about the barn. Everything was in darkness. He'd moved out of the house the day before to make the Hamiltons feel more comfortable. If it had been up to him he would have moved on but Martha had insisted that he was still recuperating and not yet fit to travel.

Kane would not complain however as she was a wonderful cook and he hadn't eaten so well in a long time. The sheriff also wanted to see him before he rode on.

The smell of fresh hay filled his nostrils as he rolled on to his side and looked at the small slivers of silver moonlight that filtered through the cracks in the wall boards. Maybe he'd leave in a couple more days. Maybe?

Kane heard the buckskin snort and stomp his hoof out in the side corral. He froze as his ears strained to hear.

The horse made another noise and Kane said in a voice loud enough for the horse to hear, 'Keep it down. I'm awake.'

The horse went still and Kane listened intently.

At first, Kane could hear nothing and almost dismissed it, thinking that the buckskin was being its usual self. As he continued to listen, a dull rumble began to drift inside the barn.

Horses.

Kane pulled his boots on and climbed to his feet. He buckled on his Peacemaker and moved cautiously to the barn door.

By the time he reached it, the thunder of hoofs had grown louder and the snorts of hard-ridden horses were easy to hear.

Kane peered around the edge of the door and saw the outline of many riders as they approached the farm. The sight of what they carried turned his blood to ice.

Flaming torches. It was obvious that these riders intended to burn the Hamiltons out. With what he owed them for saving his life, he determined to try and prevent that from happening. Yes, he owed them at least that much.

CHAPTER 5

The riders thundered into the yard and shouted loudly. One of them rode up to the front of the house with a flaming torch and was about to project it on to the roof when a voice cracked like a whip and stopped him mid-throw.

'Let that thing go and I'll kill you!' Kane called out.

'What the hell?' exclaimed another rider.

Kane walked out into the moonlight where he was clearly visible, his cocked Peacemaker unwavering in his fist.

'Who the hell are you?'

Kane noticed that each of them wore hoods to hide their identities.

'I'm the feller who's goin' to kill you if any of you cowardly sons of bitches make a wrong move,' he said calmly.

'There's six of us,' the rider pointed out.

Jordan had left the wounded man plus two others back at the miner's shack. He'd figured that he wouldn't have much trouble with the straightforward job of burning out a homesteader.

'That's fine,' Kane replied. 'I have six bullets. One for each of you.'

The rider cast a glance to the hooded figure beside him who Kane figured for the man in charge.

There was a hushed whisper then a heavy silence. When the man's body language changed Kane prepared for what was about to happen.

The man snarled a savage curse and threw the torch to the ground. It was a decoy move, totally designed to distract the gunfighter's attention and later, Kane would curse himself that it worked.

When it hit the ground and flared up, the leader of the night riders drew his six-gun and fired.

Kane felt the slug singe the skin of his neck as it passed close. He dived to his right and came up on one knee. His Peacemaker roared to life.

He missed his intended target as another rider was in the way and the bullet took him in the shoulder. The wounded rider cried out in pain and grabbed at his saddle horn.

More guns opened up and Kane was forced to lunge through the open barn doors in retreat. He glanced around the door frame and saw a hooded rider throw a torch on to the farmhouse roof.

Kane watched as the flames began to take hold of

the dry shingle roof. He flinched when a bullet gouged splinters from the door frame of the barn. A sliver scored his cheek and drew a thin line of blood.

He fired a rewarding shot at the rider and watched him fall from the saddle.

The gunfire intensified and bullets hammered into the woodwork of the barn.

A rider came forward and threw his torch through the open loft door – the hay caught quickly and began to burn fiercely above Kane's head.

As the man retreated, Kane shot him. Now there were four, and one of them was wounded.

A rifle opened up from the house and another man fell from his horse.

They were caught in a cross-fire.

Kane stepped out into the yard from inside the barn and fired at a rider who was fighting to bring his frightened horse under control.

The bullet from the Peacemaker blew the top off his head, and sprayed blood and gore over the man nearest him.

It proved to be enough and the two remaining riders sawed on the reins of their mounts and rode them hard out of the yard.

Kane turned his attention to the burning house and saw Hamilton, his wife and daughter spill out the door. Hamilton still clutched the rifle he had used.

Once in the middle of the house yard they stopped and looked about. Hamilton dropped the rifle and put his arms around his tearful family. Together they watched as their dreams burned to the ground.

'What the hell happened?' Lance fumed.

'My brother,' Jordan replied.

Lance started. 'What?'

'Lucas was there.'

'What was he doin' there?' Lance snapped.

Jordan bit back an angry retort. 'How should I know? Would you like me to go back and ask him?'

Lance waved the question away. 'No, no.'

'Besides, we got the job done anyway.'

'And lost half of the men you hired,' Lance blustered again.

The gunfighter shrugged coldly. 'They knew the risks.'

Lance nodded. Beneath the surface, he still roiled. He'd been assured that Lucas Kane was dead.

'What do you want done next?' Jordan asked him.

'We wait and see what happens,' Lance answered. 'Then if it don't work, we hit 'em again.'

As the wagon rumbled along the main street of Buford the following morning, the Hamiltons looked a sorry sight.

Unable to save anything, they were dressed in their night clothes and the townsfolk who walked the wooden planks of the boardwalk stared at them openly.

Kane rode beside them on his buckskin and felt their pained embarrassment.

In the back of the wagon, hidden from view under a tarp were the bodies of the raiders from the night before.

Hamilton stopped the wagon outside of the Buford boarding house. He climbed down stiffly then helped his wife and daughter.

As he watched them walk inside under the curious gazes of the bystanders, Kane said, 'Go with them, Brock. I'll take care of the wagon.'

Hamilton stared at Kane, his mind still numb from the previous night's events. He shook his head. 'No. I need to see the sheriff.'

'I'll take care of it,' Kane assured him. 'Go and look after your family. If the sheriff wants to see you he'll come callin'.'

Hamilton's gaze fell on to the wagon and its grisly unseen cargo.

'Are you sure?'

'Yeah.'

Kane watched him go. He tied the buckskin behind the wagon then climbed into the seat. He moved the wagon further down the street and pulled up in front of the undertaker's false-fronted parlour.

The hawk-faced man must have had a sixth sense for dead bodies because he appeared at the top of the boardwalk before Kane had a chance to step up.

'My name is Merrill, sir,' he introduced himself.

'How can I help you?'

Kane cast a thumb over his shoulder and said, 'There are four dead men in the back of the wagon. They'll need takin' care of.'

Merrill raised his eyebrows, surprised. 'Four?'

'Yeah.'

'Ahh, who'll be paying for them?' the undertaker stammered.

'Buford Lance,' Kane replied without hesitation. He was certain that the rancher was behind it.

'Very well.'

'Is it possible to get someone to clean out the wagon too?' the gunfighter asked. 'It's a little messy back there.'

'Weelll. . . .' Merrill hesitated.

'I'll pay for it,' Kane assured him.

'It'll be taken care of.'

'Thanks.'

Kane tied the buckskin to the hitch-rail outside the jail and walked across the boardwalk to the door. He turned the handle and pushed his way through the opening.

Inside, he found Brooks talking to another man. The expressions on their faces were very serious and Brooks was a little surprised to see that it was Kane who entered.

'It's started,' Brooks said flatly.

'I know.'

Brooks looked puzzled. 'What do you mean you know?'

'There was a bunch of riders hit the Hamilton place last night,' Kane explained. 'I just rode into town with 'em.'

Brooks' face showed concern. 'Are they OK?'

'In a fashion,' Kane allowed. 'They lost their home and their barn though. The riders burned 'em.'

'Damn it. They weren't hurt in any way?'

Kane shook his head. 'No. But between me and Hamilton we gave 'em somethin' to think about. They rode in with six and left four behind. Their bodies are over at the undertaker's.'

'They hit us yesterday,' the other man in the room said.

Brooks gestured to him and introduced them. 'This is Ernest Hughes. He arrived yesterday with the homesteaders. They were hit in the afternoon. They lost three men dead and some others were wounded. Hughes, this feller is Lucas Kane.'

Kane's grim expression said it all as he looked at Hughes. The recognition was evident in the homesteader's face. 'Were they wearin' hoods?'

Hughes nodded. 'Yes. They just swept down off a hill overlookin' our camp and came in shootin' recklessly. They shot our stock, including the chickens. We're just thankful none of the women and children were hurt.'

'Apparently the feller leadin' 'em wore black,'

Brooks put in. 'Anyone spring to mind?'

'It don't take a genius to figure it out,' Kane allowed.

'Who?'

Both Kane and Brooks turned to Hughes. It was the sheriff who answered.

'Jordan Kane.'

The change on Hughes' face was visible. 'You mean the. . . ?'

'Yeah,' said Brooks.

The homesteader's eyes flicked to Kane. 'But your last name is. . . .'

The gunfighter nodded. 'Yeah.'

'So what. . . ?'

'He's my brother,' Kane filled in.

'Oh lord,' Hughes whispered.

'The problem is that nobody saw their faces so it can't be proved in a court of law,' Brooks pointed out.

'Then how do you actually know that it was your brother?' Hughes asked.

'Because I was brought here to do the job that he started yesterday,' Kane told him evenly. 'See that you homesteaders don't stay.'

Hughes' eyes snapped across to Brooks, who nodded.

'But what about the law? We have that on our side. The land we intend to settle on is ours. We have legal title to it.'

'That's only if you live there for five years and improve it,' Brooks pointed out.

'And the feller who wants it back aims to see that you ain't there that long,' Kane added. 'Law or no law.'

Brooks walked around behind his scarred hard-wood desk and sat in his chair. He thought for a moment before he looked up at Hughes.

'Go back to your wagons,' the sheriff told him. 'All of you stay grouped together for a few days and I'll see what I can do.'

'Sheriff, we didn't come all this way. . . .' Hughes' voice trailed off as Brooks held up a placating hand.

'Just give me a few days.'

'Well, OK then.'

The two men watched Hughes leave and when the door was shut, Kane turned to Brooks.

'What are you aimin' to do?'

Brooks stood up and moved to a small pot-bellied stove where a coffee pot simmered.

'Coffee?' he asked, dodging the question.

'Sure, why not?'

Kane watched as he poured two mugs of the steaming-hot black liquid.

Brooks handed him a mug then pointed at a spare chair. 'Take a seat and let's talk some.'

Kane sat down and took a sip of the bitter coffee.

'Did you recognize any of them fellers you brought in?' Brooks inquired.

'Only one. A gunman named Kemp. Had a name for workin' outside the law.'

'I've heard of him,' the sheriff allowed.

'What are you goin' to do?' Kane asked again.

'I was hopin' to give you a job.'

CHAPTER 6

Kane laughed. 'You can't be serious?'

Brooks shrugged his shoulders.

'Hell,' Kane cursed. 'You are serious.'

Brooks sat forward in his seat. 'Damn right I'm serious. Do you really think I can do this on my own? I'll get burned down quick smart if I try goin' up against your brother.'

'What about the marshals?'

'It'd be all over by the time they arrived.'

'So you want me to take the job and go up against my own brother,' Kane guessed.

'No, not quite,' Brooks said unconvincingly. 'I think with you on the other side of the fence, Jordan might think twice.'

'Well I hate to poke holes in your theory, Brooks, but I'm pretty sure it was my brother who put a bullet in me.'

'I need your help, Kane,' Brooks pleaded. 'I can't do it on my own. I ain't good enough.'

'No, sheriff, I plan on ridin' out just as soon as I see that the Hamiltons are fine.'

'What about next time?'

'What about it?'

'What happens the next time those riders hit the homesteaders?' Brooks asked him. 'You know they ain't goin' to leave. What happens when the shootin' starts up again? Maybe a woman gets shot or, heaven forbid, a child catches a stray bullet?'

Kane was silent.

'What if next time it's the Hamilton's little girl?'

Kane knew he was right. He didn't want to think about it, but Brooks was right.

'Hell,' Kane muttered. 'You talk a good fight, Brooks, I'll give you that. You know at the end of all this that I'm goin' to have to go up against my brother don't you?'

Brooks nodded sombrely. 'Yeah, it is almost certain. But he's a killer. Plain and simple. You and I both know it.'

In a way, Kane had always known the time would come when he'd have to face Jordy over smoking Colts. Even though he didn't want to. But Jordy would never let it go because he wanted to be the best.

'What is it that you want me to do?'

'Go and see if you can track them hooded riders

66

back to whichever rock they crawled out from under,' Brooks told him. 'There were nine of 'em that hit the homesteaders' wagons and you killed four you say last night?'

Kane nodded.

'So that still leaves a few of 'em. I'll find a couple of men to go with you. They won't be much with a gun but they'll see it through.'

The gunfighter shook his head. 'I'll go alone.'

'OK,' said Brooks, understanding. He then opened a drawer in his desk and fished out a deputy sheriff's badge. 'I best make it all legal then.'

Once the formalities were over and the badge pinned in place, Kane fingered the unfamiliar object on his chest then looked at Brooks.

'What is it you're goin' to do while I'm gone?'

'I might have a word to Lance.' Brooks could see the thoughts going through the gunfighter's mind and reassured him. 'It won't be nothing too much. I'll just let him know that I know that he's behind it.'

'Maybe I should come with you,' Kane suggested.

'Don't worry none about me,' Brooks said. 'I'll be fine.'

'Just watch your back then.'

'Always do.'

The mid-afternoon sun was still hot when Brooks' horse splashed through the stream and followed the trail up the small cut to the B-L connected ranch house. He rode into the yard and up to the front of the house.

There were a couple of hands doing maintenance in the yard as he rode up. Foreman Chuck was standing on the verandah in front of him when he finally dismounted.

'What brings you out here, Brooks?' he asked abruptly.

'I've come to see your boss.'

'You're wastin' your time. He ain't here. He's out on the range.'

'Let him come in, Chuck.'

Brooks shifted his gaze and saw that Buford Lance stood in the open doorway.

The sheriff was about to put his foot on the first step when another man appeared beside the rancher. He was dressed in black and Brooks knew instantly that this was the infamous Jordan Kane.

He hesitated briefly but continued to climb the stairs, his boots clunked with every step.

The Buford sheriff followed them inside the house and into the plush living room.

'What do you want, Brooks?' Lance asked in a no-nonsense voice. 'Make it quick. I have no time to be wastin' bandyin' words with you. I'm busy.'

'It would seem so.'

'What's that supposed to mean?' Lance snapped.

Brooks shifted his gaze to Jordan Kane, who graced him with a cold smile.

'I had a visit from a homesteader from the wagon train that's shifted on to the free graze range along Cottonwood Creek,' he explained. 'It seems they were attacked by hooded riders not long after they set up.'

'So?' Lance's reply was flippant.

'He said the feller leadin' 'em wore black clothes.'

'Could've been anyone,' Lance said. 'Might have been rustlers. They've been gettin' around. I've been meanin' to come see you about them.'

Brooks shook his head. 'No. They shot some of their stock and some of their people. But that's not all. Seems some riders, I'm assuming the same ones, hit the Hamilton spread last night and burned 'em out.'

Once again Brooks looked at Jordan Kane. 'Your brother brought them in, along with four bodies. He knew one of 'em. Feller by the name of Kemp.'

There was no reaction from Jordan.

Brooks continued. 'You wouldn't know anythin' about Lucas bein' bushwhacked the other day, would you?'

And there it was. A momentary flicker in the killer's eyes was enough to tell the sheriff that what he'd just heard about his brother was news to him.

Then it was gone.

'No? Anyway,' he turned back to Lance. 'I just thought I'd let you know to keep an eye out just in case.'

'We've had no trouble here,' Lance said impatiently. 'If there ain't anythin' else I have work to do.'

'No, nothin' else,' Brooks told him. 'But if you do, you can let me or my new deputy know.'

'Deputy? What deputy?' Lance snapped.

'I hired a new one because of all this trouble startin' up with these hooded riders. I can't do it on my own,' Brooks replied.

'Who is it?' Lance asked.

Brooks smiled. 'Lucas Kane.'

Lance's eyes snapped across to Jordan then quickly back to Brooks. Inside, the rancher seethed at the failure of Concho Bell once more.

'Why would he help you?' Lance sneered.

'Maybe because he wants to find the feller who bushwhacked him. Or perhaps it's become personal now after the riders burned down the home of the homesteaders who took him in when he was wounded.'

Brooks let his words sink in before he added, 'Oh well, I'll be off now. I can show myself out.'

When he was gone, Jordan Kane's icy gaze settled on Lance.

'Do you know anythin' about Lucas bein' ambushed, Lance?'

The rancher shook his head.

'No,' he lied. 'Could be one of his many enemies has caught up with him.'

'When I find out who it was they'll be sorry,'

Jordan growled. 'I want to be the one to kill my brother. Nobody else.'

'How about I give you another job to do instead?'

'What?'

'I want Brooks out of the way,' Lance elaborated. 'He came out here because he knows I'm behind it all and he wanted to let me know that he knows. And maybe with him gone, your brother might ride on.'

'How do you want me to do it?'

'Quietly if possible.'

'Consider it done.'

The hooded riders hadn't bothered to cover or even attempted to hide their tracks. Perhaps it was arrogance or just sheer stupidity. It did, however, make it easier for Kane to track them. He supposed they figured that no one would come after them.

Then he thought about Jordy and guessed that his brother figured himself to be invincible and wouldn't care if anybody did.

The trail had led Kane into the foothills to the base of the mountains. There he followed the trail alongside a rocky bottomed stream. The far bank rose up through tall spruce trees and stopped at the foot of high, grey-faced peaks. Lush green grass grew along the edge of the water and small wild flowers broke up the sea of green.

Overhead, a blue sky was dotted with leaden clouds.

The trail cut away from the stream and followed a dry gulch for a mile or so before it climbed a tree-lined ridge.

As Kane moved higher, he broke out of the trees. On a bench at the bottom of a scree slope, surrounded by rock, grass, and a few aspen, was a shack. By the looks of the workings up the slope from the building, he assumed that it was probably an old mining shack.

There was a patched-up corral beside the shack with rails made of aspen. Four horses were enclosed and paced around.

'Unless I missed my guess,' Kane murmured, 'I'd say I've found what I was looking for.'

He eased back into the trees and tied the buckskin to a low branch. Then he crept forward where he could see the shack. He didn't want to ride in until he knew what he would have to deal with.

Kane sat and watched the shack for an hour. No one left or entered.

The buckskin whickered and Kane instantly dropped his hand to the butt of his Peacemaker. The dry triple-click of a gun hammer being eared back stayed his hand.

A harsh voice warned, 'Pull that and you're a dead man.'

Slowly Kane eased his hand away from the six-gun. Inwardly he cursed himself for allowing the man to get the drop on him.

'Turn around,' the man ordered.

With raised hands, Kane turned to face his captor.

'Well I'll be, Lucas Kane,' the man sneered.

Kane stared at him. The speaker was a two-bit gunman from around Trinidad called Dexter Jones. He had a square-jawed face with buck-teeth and ice-blue eyes.

'Howdy Dex, fancy seein' you here,' Kane said. 'Bat Masterson run you out of Trinidad?'

'Jordy said you was about,' Dex told him. He pointed at the star pinned to his shirt. 'Didn't say anythin' about that, though.'

Kane shrugged. 'Are you boys goin' to come in quietly?'

The gunman frowned. 'What?'

'I just want to know if you and them other three in the shack are goin' to come in quietly,' he explained. 'I know one of them is wounded because I put the lead in him myself.'

Dex smiled and gave the gunfighter a look that told him that the man thought he was crazy.

'You do know that you're starin' down the barrel of a cocked six-gun, right?'

'Yeah, but I figure that you ain't goin' to shoot me, Dex,' the gunfighter opined. 'You see if Jordy knows I'm still about, which you said he does, he ain't goin' to want you shootin' me. I'm guessin' that he said that if any one of you fellers shoot me, instead of him, he'd kill you. You see, Jordy wants to be the best. And to do that, he has to kill me. Am I right?'

Dex was quiet.

Kane nodded. 'Uh-huh, I thought so. So it seems to me that you have yourself a dilemma.'

'A what? Is that even a word?' asked Dex, pulling a face.

Kane relaxed and let out a long, even breath.

'It means that you are in two minds about what to do with me, Dex,' he explained. 'Which is a bad place to be for men like us who live by the gun. Because while you are still thinkin' about what to do I can. . . .'

By the time Dex realized what was happening it was too late. Kane's right hand had dropped and come up full of belching Peacemaker.

The hammer fell on the .45 calibre cartridge and the slug smashed into Dex's chest. His mouth flew open at the shock of the impact but no sound escaped and a large blossom of red appeared.

The six-gun fell from lifeless fingers and thudded on the matted grass at his feet. Dex slipped to his knees and toppled sideways on to his back. His sightless eyes stared up at the blue sky above.

Kane shook his head. The shot was a dead giveaway that someone else was up here, and he still had to get the rest of them out of the shack.

He moved back into some cover to think about the situation. He decided that his best course of action was to wait until after dark. It wasn't a great plan but maybe he could get them under the cover of darkness without getting himself killed.

CHAPTER 7

Three hours after the sun had sunk behind the great mountain peaks of the Sangre de Cristo Range there was still no sign of Kane. Brooks wasn't all that worried because he was sure the man could look after himself. He'd just have to wait patiently for his return.

Brooks sighed and pushed his empty plate away across his desk. A few brown streaks of gravy were all that remained of his meal of steak and potato. He stood and walked to the gun rack on the wall and took down a sawed-off coach gun.

He returned to his desk and took shells from the top drawer. He broke open the gun and fed them into the twin barrels. He snapped them closed and looked at the gun in his hands.

He wouldn't normally carry it on his rounds but he had a nagging feeling that wouldn't go away.

Outside the jail, the main street was lit by intermittently placed kerosene lanterns. Long shadows were cast by inanimate objects.

Brooks' boots sounded unusually loud as he stepped out on to the boardwalk.

It was a clear night and the stars twinkled in the dark sky. The air held a slight chill but in all, it was quite pleasant.

'Evenin', Tom.'

Brooks spun sideways towards the voice and breathed a sigh of relief that the speaker was only the local hostler, Frank Redmond.

'Evenin', Frank,' he managed to get out, annoyed at himself for jumping at shadows.

'Sorry, Sheriff,' Redmond apologized. 'I didn't mean to startle you.'

'Gettin' jumpy in my old age,' Brooks said, as he attempted to make light of the comment.

'Is that why you're carryin' that cannon around?' the hostler asked, and nodded at the coach gun.

'Just in case.'

Brooks watched Redmond continue on his way then turned and walked off in the opposite direction.

As he went, Brooks mentally ticked off the businesses. The drug store, the laundry run by Xoa Ping, the assayer's office, land office and the barber shop.

Further on was the Nugget saloon. Brooks paused and peered in over the bat-wing doors. The place was close to capacity and the noise that emanated from the smoke-filled room was raucous.

Brooks continued on to the end of the main street then crossed over and walked the boardwalk on the opposite side.

This time, he passed the gunsmith's shop, Sigurd's blacksmith shop, and the newly transformed drapery. Beyond that was the Cattleman's Bank, Lisa's Kitchen and the hotel.

As he walked past the alley between Horton's dry goods store and the telegraph office, he heard a strange noise coming from the darkness beyond.

Brooks stopped and listened intently. He heard the noise again. It sounded like a muffled moan. Something a man would make when hurt.

The sheriff eared back the hammers on the shotgun and stepped cautiously into the mouth of the alley.

'Hello?'

Another moan.

Brooks edged forward slowly deeper into the darkness, his left shoulder all but rubbed against the plank wall of the telegraph office.

'Hello?'

This time, there was silence.

When the sheriff reached the end of the alley he almost fell over a prone form that lay across the exit. A small sliver of light cast from inside Widow Baker's house was enough to prevent his fall.

'What the hell?' Brooks muttered as he knelt down

beside the unconscious man.

As he rolled him over, the light shone on the bloodied face of the hostler, Frank Redmond.

'Hell Frank, what happened?' Brooks whispered.

Even though the hostler couldn't hear him, the sheriff said reassuringly, 'I'll go and get Doc Reed. Be back in a moment.'

Brooks stood and turned hurriedly towards the main street only to be faced with the dark shadow of another man. Before he could say or do anything, the stranger stepped forward and drove a knife between the sheriff's ribs. The sudden explosive departure of breath from Brooks' lungs was followed by a burning pain in his chest and weakness as his life began to ebb.

A second thrust as hard as the first completed the killer's intent and the coach gun dropped from Brooks' grasp. It thudded dully at the sheriff's feet.

His knees buckled and he slid to the ground beside the unconscious Redmond.

Jordan Kane bent down and wiped the blade of his knife clean on Brooks' pant leg. Then as he sheathed it, he smiled.

Lucas Kane decided that the time was right and moved out of the trees with an armful of dry twigs and sticks, which he needed if his plan was to work. He approached from the blind side of the shack. Bent low he moved cautiously, aware that if the outlaws emerged now he would be caught in the open.

None of them had poked their heads out after the shooting but he knew they would remain vigilant because Dex hadn't returned.

When he reached the shack, he paused and listened intently. He heard nothing from within and proceeded to set the sticks against the dry wood of the shack wall. Once done, he reached into his pocket for the matches he always carried.

The first one flared and went out. The second stayed alight long enough to get it amongst the smaller, dry twigs. Once the pile had caught, he stood back and called out to those inside.

'I smell smoke,' Morg said and lifted his head like a wolf testing the air.

'I don't smell nothin',' Cutter said.

'I tell you I smell it,' Morg insisted. 'Do you suppose he's still out there? Maybe he's tryin' to burn us out.'

'You're dreamin'.'

'But Cutter. . . .'

'Just shut up and check on Bert,' Cutter snapped and turned back towards the window.

Bert was asleep on the bunk and had been since Cutter had dug the bullet from his back last night. Morgan, on the other hand, had done nothing but moan about his flesh wound.

'Hey you in the shack! Come on out!'

'Who's that?' Morg whispered.

'Who the hell do you think?' Cutter said bitterly.

'What do you want?' he called out.

'You fellers best come on out if you don't want to burn in there,' Kane told Cutter.

'I told you I smelled smoke,' Morg said, his anxiety levels raised at the prospect of dying.

Cutter drew his Colt and called out, 'Who the hell are you, stranger?'

'Lucas Kane,' Kane answered.

'Oh hell,' moaned Morg.

'Was that you at the homesteader's place last night Kane?' Cutter asked.

'Yeah.'

'What happens if we do come out?'

'For one thing, you won't burn alive,' Kane called out. 'But you will be taken back to town to stand trial.'

'Don't much like that idea, Kane.'

'It's all you have. Take it or leave it.'

Cutter thought briefly but the smoke began to fill his nostrils as the fire took hold of the old hut.

'All right, Kane. We're comin' out.'

'Unarmed or I'll shoot you down,' Kane warned him.

'All right.'

Outside, Kane waited for the men to appear. His

81

hand rested on the holstered Peacemaker.

The door opened and two men emerged supporting a third. Once in the open they stopped and looked at Kane.

'What now?' Cutter asked.

'Put your friend down and saddle up them horses. Unless you want to walk to town.'

'Go to hell, Kane,' Cutter snarled loudly and brought his arm out from behind the man he was carrying. As the six-gun came up, Cutter thumbed back the hammer and the sound alerted Kane to the threat.

The Peacemaker leapt from its holster and roared loudly. The bullet smashed into Cutter's chest before his gun could level at Kane. He cried out in pain and fell to the ground.

'Don't shoot!' Morgan shouted, and raised his free hand up in the air.

'Don't move,' Kane ordered and walked over to check on Cutter. He needn't have bothered because the outlaw was dead.

Kane stood up and turned to Morgan and Bert. 'Your friend is dead and unless you both want to end up the same way, I suggest that you do exactly what I say.'

CHAPTER 8

It was around noon the following day when Kane rode into the main street of Buford leading the four outlaws' horses. The last two had the bodies of Dex and Cutter draped over them. The next one carried the wounded Bert, hunched forward over the saddle horn.

Directly behind Kane was the still-moaning Morg.

As he moved along the street, curious onlookers gathered and followed his progress. By the time he eased to a stop outside the jail, he'd drawn a sizeable crowd.

After he dismounted, a lone figure pushed through the crowd towards him and he recognized Brock Hamilton.

'Can you give me a hand to get that wounded feller off?' Kane asked him.

'Are these the men that burned my place?' Hamilton asked, a hard edge to his voice.

'Yes.'

Hamilton's face screwed up with rage as he reached up to pull the wounded Bert from the back of the horse.

'Brock!' Kane snapped. 'Do it nice and easy. I know you got no love for these fellers but leave it to the court to decide what to do with them.'

'Says the man who lives by the gun,' Hamilton snarled back.

Kane knew he was right. What he'd just said made him sound like a hypocrite. He turned to the crowd and picked out a slim man with black hair.

'Can you go and find the doctor?'

'Sure,' he said and disappeared into the mass.

Kane turned back to Hamilton. 'Are you goin' to help me or will I just get the sheriff to?'

Hamilton opened his mouth to speak but closed it again. Murmurs rippled through the crowd and Kane frowned, perceiving that something was up.

'What's goin' on?'

His gaze burned into Hamilton and the homesteader dropped his eyes briefly. When he looked up, the expression on his face had changed noticeably.

'Sheriff Brooks is dead, Lucas,' Hamilton informed him.

'He what?'

'He's dead,' Hamilton repeated.

'Damn it,' Kane cursed. 'Help me get these fellers inside, Brock, and tell me what happened.'

Once Kane had locked Morg up and shown the

doctor to Bert's cell, he returned to the jail office and sat on the edge of the desk.

'Tell me what you know, Brock.'

Hamilton took a deep breath and began to elaborate on the events of the morning. 'They found Sheriff Brooks this mornin'. It wasn't long after dawn. Whoever found him found Frank Redmond, the hostler, beside him. Frank had been wailed on real bad and was still out to it. Brooks had been stabbed.

'Who found him?' Kane asked.

Hamilton shook his head. 'I don't know.'

'Did anybody hear or see anythin'?'

'Not that I know of.'

Kane was about to ask Hamilton another question when the doctor came in from the cells.

He was a young man, maybe middle thirties and yet to suffer the rigours of hard frontier life. His name was Ezra Stone.

'He'll live,' he told them. 'Long enough to hang anyway.'

'That's somethin' I guess,' Kane sighed. 'Tell me about Brooks and Redmond, Doc.'

'Not much to tell really. Brooks was stabbed twice and Redmond was beaten up pretty bad with a gun-barrel.'

'Has he talked at all?'

Stone shook his head. 'Not much. He didn't see who did it to him if that's what you're getting at.'

85

'I've got a good idea who did it, Doc,' Kane said grimly. 'Provin' it might be a whole other issue.'

Before more could be said, the jail house door swung open and a man dressed in a black suit entered. He was, however, not alone. Behind him were Buford Lance and the cold, smiling Jordan Kane.

'I think you two best leave,' Kane suggested to Hamilton and Stone. 'I'll deal with this.'

Without a word the two men left the office and closed the door behind them.

Kane turned his flinty gaze on the three men and asked, 'What do you want?'

'What, no formalities?' asked Lance. His voice dripped with sarcasm.

'Mighty confident with my brother standin' behind you, huh Lance?'

'Aah, Mr Kane . . .' the man in the suit started tentatively. 'My name is Peters. I'm the mayor of Buford.'

Kane noticed the beads of nervous perspiration on the man's brow.

'What brings you here, Mayor?' Kane asked him.

'Umm. . . . By now you would be aware that Sheriff Brooks was stabbed to death last night.'

Kane nodded. 'I am.'

Peters fidgeted nervously and his tongue darted across his dry lips. 'In light of it all, the town council held a meeting this morning and decided to install a

BROTHERS OF THE GUN

new sheriff. Can't be without one with all this trouble
going on, can we?'

'It would seem like the thing to do,' Kane agreed
suspiciously.

'Right. So we found a man for the job and he's
going to start straight away,' Peters explained. 'The
only issue is that he won't require a deputy. So I'm
afraid your services won't be needed.'

'Does the new man have any idea what he's takin'
on?' Kane asked.

Peters gave him a nervous smile. 'Yes, I'm quite
sure he does. You see the new sheriff is . . . aah. . . .'

'Oh hell, it pains me to watch it,' Lance's voice cut
across the stammering mayor. 'What he's tryin' to tell
you is that the new sheriff is your brother and he sure
as hell don't need help from you.'

Kane stared at Jordy's smiling face and knew
without a doubt that he was solely responsible for the
murder of Brooks. Finding proof would be nigh on
impossible, especially now that he had no official
powers of investigation.

'So this is how it's goin' to be?' Kane said to Lance.
'You're goin' to try and manipulate the law somehow
to move the homesteaders off their land.'

Lance's eyes blazed. 'It's my land.'

'They have . . .'

'They have nothing!' the rancher shrieked. 'The
land is mine! I took it and I kept it. I have blood
invested in that range and no damn sodbuster is

87

goin' to take it away from me.'

Kane shook his head in bewilderment. How could you argue with a man like that?

'It might be best if you left town, Lucas,' Jordan advised him, his fingers flexed over the ivory gun-butt of his right side Colt. 'Can't have you hangin' around causin' trouble in our peaceful town.'

Without taking his eyes from his brother, Kane reached up and unpinned the badge he wore. He tossed it on to the scarred desk where it landed with a dull thunk.

'Maybe you're right, Jordy,' Kane allowed. 'Maybe I will leave town.'

The two men watched Kane leave, followed by the mayor. Once the door was closed they looked at each other, surprised that their plan had gone so smoothly.

'That was easy,' Lance allowed. 'He just turned tail and left. Didn't even give a yelp. Some "Gun King".'

Jordan Kane wasn't convinced.

'Maybe too easy. He's up to somethin',' he said, suspicious of what had transpired. 'Like you said, Lance, he gave in far too quickly. I think that badge was weighing too heavy on him. And I also think he's glad to be rid of it. He ain't goin' nowhere.'

Lance thought for a moment then said, 'I'll have him followed. Just in case you're right.'

'You do that,' Jordan said. 'Now, what do you have planned for the homesteaders?'

'Now you're the sheriff, I want you to lean on all the shopkeepers in town and tell 'em to sell nothin' to them damned squatters. Tell 'em if they do, I'll bring my whole crew to town and burn their shops down around their ears with them inside.'

'I can do that.'

'Good. Make sure they understand.'

Brock Hamilton stopped Kane before he'd gone fifty feet towards the outskirts of town.

'Where are you goin'? he asked the gunfighter. 'More to the point, where is the badge?'

'I gave it back,' Kane told him.

'But why?'

'Let's just say I'm better off without it.'

'So where are you goin'?' Hamilton asked again, aware that Kane hadn't answered his question.

'I'm leavin' town.'

'Are you comin' back?'

'What the hell is this?' Kane snapped impatiently. 'Twenty damn questions? I'm leavin' and that's that. The sheriff is dead so I'm out of a job.'

'The homesteaders need you. We need you,' Hamilton pleaded. 'Without you, we don't stand a chance.'

'You never stood a chance anyway,' Kane said coldly. 'Look, I'm grateful to you and your wife for helpin' me, I really am. But you need to take your family and get gone from here, sooner rather than

89

later if you value your lives.'

The look of disdain that Hamilton gave him cut deeper than any bullet ever could. 'Thanks for nothin', gunslinger.'

Without any further words, Hamilton spun on his heel and stalked angrily away.

Kane kneed his horse forward and kept riding out of town. When the buildings had dropped away, he urged the buckskin into a canter, eager to put it all behind him.

There was nothing he could do for them. The home-steaders were bucking a stacked deck. Besides, if he stayed, he would eventually have to go up against Jordy and he wasn't exactly sure he wanted to do that.

As he rode, a feeling of foreboding pervaded his senses that Brock Hamilton was about to do some-thing very stupid, from which there would be no coming back. His thoughts went to Martha and Elsie who would be left all alone, unable to fend for them-selves.

A mile from town the trail forked. The left fork would take him to the town of Broken Flats. Instead, he took the right.

CHAPTER 9

The colour of the landscape changed, casting hues of purple and orange as the sun sank lower in the sky and gradually dropped behind the distant mountains.

Ernest Hughes was on lookout when a rider crested the hill. He shouted a warning to the other homesteaders and they scattered. Women and children sought shelter under the wagons while the menfolk snatched up rifles and six-guns, prepared to do battle if it came to that.

Hughes noted the casual demeanour of the rider who rocked steadily with the smooth motion of the buckskin horse. When he drew closer, Hughes could see that it was Lucas Kane.

'Hold your fire!' Hughes shouted and moved out from behind the shelter of the wagon.

Kane drew up and waited for an invitation to step down.

'What brings you out here, Kane?' the homesteader asked.

'I came to warn you, you're headed for trouble.'

'We've been in trouble ever since we got here,' Hughes informed him.

Kane looked about as the homesteaders started to gather around. At first, it was just the men with their guns but slowly the women and children emerged.

'Well, trouble just got a whole lot worse,' Kane said grimly. 'Sheriff Brooks is dead.'

Hughes couldn't hide the shock on his face, 'No. How?'

'He was stabbed last night while I was out trackin' down the hooded riders who attacked your camp and the Hamilton spread,' Kane explained.

'You what?'

'How about you let me get down from here and I can fill you in from the beginnin'?' Kane suggested.

'Yes, of course. Climb on down and follow me.'

Hughes' face blanched instantly when Kane informed him that Jordy was the new sheriff of Buford.

'Oh, lord,' he gasped out. 'What shall we do now? With Brooks gone and your brother as sheriff, Lance will stop at nothing to get us off this land.'

'Just stay calm,' Kane told him. 'No one's done anythin' yet. What are your plans for the next few days?'

'We're goin' to take up our quarter sections,' a slim man put in. 'Or we were.'

'How about you all work together,' Kane suggested. 'Start building one homestead at a time. Just for now.'

'But why?' Hughes asked.

'Safety in numbers,' the gunfighter explained. 'If one of you needs to go to town, five go. If you need to cut wood, take another three with you so nobody gets caught out alone. Do you get my meanin'?'

'Yes,' Hughes nodded.

'Some of us could go to town in the mornin' to get lumber so we can start buildin',' the thin man said.

'No. You don't need to,' Kane said reassuringly. 'Take a look around you. See all these tree-lined hills and ridges? There's all the lumber you'll need. Have any of you built a log cabin before?'

'I have,' answered a tall, broad-shouldered man, listening from the back of the circle.

'For the moment, that's all you'll need to get started. They're solid and it'll be a roof over your head. At least, until this blows over.'

They all nodded in agreement, happy with the suggestion.

'We could sure use your help, Kane,' Hughes admitted. 'We couldn't pay you much but we might be able to scrape some money together.'

'I'll stay, Hughes,' Kane told him. 'But don't worry about the money. This is one job I'll do for free.'

'Where did he go?' Lance asked of his foreman Chuck Lane, as he passed him a glass of brandy.

'Cottonwood Creek range,' Chuck confirmed.

'Damn that man!' Lance shouted and threw his half-full glass at the living room fireplace where it shattered into tiny shards. 'His brother was right. He didn't leave after all.'

'Nope. In fact, he seemed to be organisin' 'em,' Chuck commented.

'Son of a bitch,' Lance cursed. 'He just continues to be a problem. Listen, Chuck, I know it's dark out but I want you to ride out to the line shack and get Concho for me. Tell him I want to see him.'

Chuck nodded. 'Sure thing boss.'

Lance watched Chuck leave, then turned towards the map on the wall.

'And this time, Concho, you'd best earn your damned money.'

Mid-morning saw the arrival of Chuck and Concho back at the ranch. As Lance sat and waited for them to enter the room, a longcase clock chimed and signalled the top of the hour.

'Mind tellin' me what's goin' on?' Concho asked as he barged in. 'Your man here wouldn't say a word. I was startin' to think he'd gone mute.'

Lance stared at him levelly asked, 'When you took

care of Kane, did you check the body?'

Concho shrugged. 'Wasn't any real need to.'

The rancher repeated the question, this time, his voice carried a hint of menace. 'Did . . . you . . . check . . . the . . . body? Answer the question, damn it.'

The gunfighter's eyes flared. 'No. Don't push me, Lance.'

'I'll push you as far as I damn well want,' Lance shot back.

'Especially when I pay for a job and it doesn't get done!'

'What do you mean, doesn't get done?' Concho demanded. 'I shot the son of a bitch didn't I? He's damn well dead.'

'No, he's not.'

'He sure as hell is,' Concho snapped. 'When I kill someone, they stay dead.'

'Since you've been holed up in that line shack, I'll excuse your ignorance,' Lance said in a condescending tone. 'But Kane is very much alive and is being a thorn in my side.'

Concho shook his head, unable to believe what he'd been told. Finally, he asked, 'What do you want me to do?'

'I want you to clean up your damned mess. I want Kane gone.'

'Why don't you set the Prince against him?'

'He's takin' care of business for me in town,'

Lance explained.

'Besides, it's your mess and you've been paid to get rid of him.'

'Where is he?'

'He's holed up with the homesteaders over on the Cottonwood Creek range,' Lance told him.

'Fine, I'll go and take care of it now.'

The rancher nodded. 'Good. There is one more thing. When you've done it, keep riding and don't come back. Your services are no longer required.'

As Lance issued his final order to Concho, Hughes found Kane hooking a team up to a bundle of logs. The stand of pines they were cutting sat on a hill which overlooked the site of the first homestead.

He climbed down from his bay horse with a look of concern on his face.

Kane knew that whatever was coming couldn't be good.

'The group that went to town for supplies struck a problem, Kane,' Hughes growled. 'Not one shop-keeper would sell them anything that was on the list.'

'Sounds to me Lance has ordered them not to,' Kane surmised.

'But surely they wouldn't do that because he told them to.'

'He wouldn't have done the tellin' directly,' the gunfighter said. 'He would've had Jordy talk to 'em.'

'What are we goin' to do?' Hughes asked worriedly.

'Nothin',' Kane told him. 'He wants you all to give up. Show him that you don't intend to.'

'Then he'll send more riders against us.'

The gunfighter nodded. 'More than likely. The question you need to ask yourself, and this goes for all of the homesteaders, is are you prepared to fight for what is yours? If you ain't, you may as well leave now. Because it's quite possible more of you will die before this is done.'

It was a bleak prediction but Hughes knew that what Kane said was true.

With all hands pitched in, the work on the new homestead progressed steadily that day. Kane had posted lookouts on two of the surrounding hills to prevent being taken by surprise. It was the lookout to the east who spotted the rider first and fired a warning shot.

Homesteaders scattered and prepared to fight, found cover and took up weapons.

Everyone except Kane. He stood out in the open and waited to see what would happen next. When the lone rider swung into view, the gunfighter breathed a sigh of relief.

The rider approached at a steady pace and as he drew near, Kane recognized him as Concho Bell.

Concho drew up short and pushed his hat back. 'Howdy, Kane.'

Kane nodded. 'Concho. I guess I don't have to ask

why you're here.'

'Guess not,' he allowed. 'Although I am surprised that you're still alive. I thought I killed you the first time.'

'That was you?'

'Yeah.'

'So here you are back to finish the job,' Kane stated.

'Mind if I climb down?'

'Go ahead. Just keep your hand clear of that six-gun of yours.'

Concho dismounted and moved away from his horse, never once taking his eyes from Kane. When he considered he'd gone far enough, he planted his feet roughly shoulder width apart.

Kane knew the reputation of the man. He was considered by some throughout the vast state of Texas to be a viable challenger for the Gun King's throne. It was one of the reasons that confused him as to why Concho had shot him from ambush.

'Who hired you to bushwhack me Concho?'

The killer smiled coldly. 'You know I ain't goin' to tell you that, Kane. It wouldn't be professional, but bushwhackin' you was my idea. Didn't really want to take any chances goin' up against you.'

'So what changed?'

'This time I have to make sure. This time, it's about pride and reputation.'

For some, that's what it was all about. Kane never

wanted the reputation, but it had sought him out. Before long, he was being touted as the undisputed Gun King.

A wave of calm washed over him as it always did right before a gunfight. It was his way of making peace should he be killed.

'Anytime you're ready, Concho,' Kane told him.

The smile left the killer's face and a look of grim determination replaced it.

There was a long drawn-out silence, a pregnant pause that hung heavily in the air. The homesteaders held a collective breath and prayed that the man they wished to be their saviour would prevail.

When it was over, those who'd been a witness would swear that there'd been no movement of Kane's gun arm. One moment it was hanging loose and the next, his hand held his Peacemaker at waist level as it roared into life.

Kane fired two shots, both of which struck Concho Bell full in the chest not two finger widths apart. His shirt blossomed red and he staggered backwards as he fought to remain on his feet. His gun barrel had just cleared leather and was still pointed at the ground.

Concho used every ounce of his waning strength to raise his six-gun, a snarl of defiance on his face. If he could just steady himself long enough. . . .

Instead, Kane's Colt roared once more and a third eye appeared in Concho's forehead. The bullet punched out the back of his skull and took bone and brain matter with it in a bright crimson spray.

The killer fell flat on his back beside his unfired six-gun.

CHAPTER 10

Hushed whispers followed Kane along the street as he led the horse with Concho Bell's corpse draped over the saddle. A number of the townsfolk were still out on the street doing last-minute chores before the sun finally sank behind the Sangre de Cristo mountains when Kane hit town.

He rode up to the jail and dismounted. He tied Concho's horse to the sturdy hitch rail and mounted back up.

'What the hell is this?' Jordan Kane asked his brother as he stepped out on to the boardwalk.

'What does it look like, Jordy?'

Jordan studied the body from his position outside the door. Though he couldn't see the dead man's face he had a good idea who it was.

'Is that Concho Bell?'

Kane nodded. 'Yeah, it's him.'

'What'd you bring him here for?'

'I thought that maybe you could tell your boss the next time he sends a gun after me, make sure he's good enough to see it through.'

'What makes you figure it was him?' Jordan asked his brother.

'Come on, Jordy,' Kane snorted. 'I ain't stupid. He's been behind everythin' that's happened so far.'

The younger Kane remained silent.

'Tell me somethin'. Did you kill Brooks or did Lance have someone else do it?'

'Does it matter, Lucas?' Jordan asked. 'Dead is dead no matter who does it.'

It pained Kane to see what his brother had become. In a way he blamed himself. Jordan had always looked up to him as a youngster and the pair were close. Now, given half the chance, Kane knew his brother would draw on him and try to kill him. Just for the title of being the best.

The gunfighter started to swing his horse away from the hitch rail when Jordan threw out the challenge. 'We could settle this here and now, Lucas.'

Kane ignored him and rode off.

'Are you scared, Lucas? Is that it?'

Looking straight ahead Kane said, 'Nope, not scared. Just not ready to kill you yet, kid.'

Jordan Kane's hand dropped to one of his Peacemakers as he fought to control the urge to shoot his brother out of the saddle.

'One day soon, Lucas!' he shouted after him. 'One

day soon!'

'Yeah, Jordy,' Kane mumbled to himself with recognition. 'One day soon.'

As the gunfighter rode out of town, Brock Hamilton stood on the boardwalk and watched him leave. There was a faint smile on his lips. Maybe there was still a chance after all, he thought.

Jordan Kane's horse thundered into the B-L connected ranch yard and almost sat down hard on its rump when his rider hauled furiously back on the reins.

Jordan left it ground hitched and stormed up the steps and across the veranda. He thrust one of the double doors open and it crashed back. He stomped along the marble floor and down the hallway until he found the room he wanted. He found Lance seated in his leather-backed chair. He drew his right side Colt, thumbed back the hammer and pointed it at the rancher.

Lance blanched noticeably but was not one to let his fear show for long.

'What in tarnation do you think you're doin'?' he asked in a raised voice. 'And put that damned gun up before you hurt someone.'

'I warned you, Lance,' Jordan said through gritted teeth. 'I told you that Lucas was mine. Yet you hire another gun to go after him.'

'You do what I pay you to do, damn it,' Lance

pointed out. 'Nothin' more.'

Jordan moved his aim so that the gaping maw of the barrel was centred on the rancher's forehead. 'I should just kill you now and be done with it.'

Twin hammers being thumbed back on a sawed off greener stayed the gunfighter's finger.

'If you don't want your head spread all round this room I suggest you leather that Colt of yours,' Chuck said calmly.

Jordan turned his head to look at the B-L connected foreman. The shotgun was pointed straight at his head.

'Just so you know, Chuck,' Jordan said casually, 'I can turn and kill you before you even think about squeezin' the trigger. Your choice.'

'Son, I been around a long time and I've heard it all before,' Chuck informed him. 'So let me tell you. If you even draw breath the wrong way I'm goin' to pull this trigger.'

Jordan looked into the foreman's eyes and knew that this was a man who could not be bluffed. If he twitched the wrong way or at the wrong time, his brains would be splattered about the room. He smiled coldly and slipped the Colt back into its holster.

If Buford Lance felt any sort of relief, he didn't show it. Instead, he asked brusquely, 'What happened?'

'Lucas turned up at the jail with Concho Bell face

down over a saddle. He said to tell you that next time send somebody better.'

'And you just let him leave?'

'I offered to settle it then and there,' Jordan explained, 'but he just rode off. Said he weren't ready to kill me yet.'

'Why didn't you just shoot him and be done with it all?' Lance snapped.

'You wouldn't understand, Lance,' Jordan answered. 'When it happens, I want everyone watching. I want there to be no doubt about who is the best.'

Lance shook his head. 'Well, that don't fix the problem we have now, does it?'

'Let me handle it,' the killer told him. 'I'm goin' to hire me some more guns. Professionals, this time, none of those tenth-rate wannabes.'

'You'd best tell me what you have in mind then.'

Over the next five days, four gunmen rode into Buford and found their way out to the B-L connected ranch.

The first man was a gunfighter by the name of Johnny Marsh. He was rail thin and had red hair.

He was a professional gun out of Utah and was said to have killed seven men in stand-up fights.

The second man to arrive went by the name of Roscoe James. He was a cold-blooded killer with a mean temper and a livid scar on his cheek, who came out of Nebraska.

Marty Collins was a New Mexican gun-for-hire. He was a flashy type who dressed in a suit and wore a derby style hat.

The remaining man was Cassidy. He originated from Kansas and was a bear of a man with deceptively fast gun-speed. One look into his ice-blue eyes told enough about the sort of killer that he was.

It was said ten men had gone down before his gun. One of his more recent jobs was a small-town sheriff trying to put a stop to a range war. Not dissimilar to the one he'd just ridden into.

Jordan Kane had travelled with Cassidy out to the ranch and they all sat around whilst they were filled in on the requirements of the job.

'How much are you payin'?' Roscoe James asked.

'I'll pay you a thousand a man,' Lance told them.

Marty Collins shook his head. 'Nope. If I'm goin' up against Lucas Kane, then I for one want more money.'

Lance was about to speak when Jordan interrupted.

'You won't be goin' up against Lucas,' he stated. 'Lucas is my concern, not yours. You lot are here for the homesteaders.'

'That's a mighty tall order considerin' that Lucas is camped out with 'em,' Cassidy pointed out. 'How do you expect us to do what you ask without tradin' lead with him?'

'I have a plan to get him out of the way,' Jordan explained to them. 'Once that has happened, then you'll be free to do what you've been hired for.'

'And what then?' asked Marsh.

'Then you'll be paid and be free to go,' Lance said abruptly.

'OK,' said Cassidy nodding. 'But if any one of us goes up against Lucas Kane and kills him, they have a bonus comin'.'

'I said. . . .' Jordan snapped but Cassidy cut him off.

'I heard you the first time, Jordan. But if it happens that we come up against him and you're not around, don't go expectin' me to tuck my tail between my legs and run away.'

Jordan just glared at Cassidy.

'Fine,' said Lance. 'If it happens, I'll pay an extra thousand.'

The big gunfighter nodded. 'Fair enough. Now, what is it we're doin'?'

One hundred miles north of Buford, in a town called Perdition, Rio Smith sat at a dark timber table with a deeply scarred surface. He was working his way through a bottle of watered-down forty-rod and currently sat and toyed with the empty shot glass.

The scrape of chair legs on bare boards sounded and a young man aged in his early twenties sat down across from him. He was an up-and-coming fast-gun and called himself Utah.

107

'Guess what?'

Rio looked at the young man and could see the excitement in his grey eyes.

'What?' he said disinterestedly.

'I think I know where Cassidy lit out for.'

'Where?'

'Buford.'

Now he had Rio's attention. 'What makes you say that?'

'Because there's a range war goin' on down there and Jordan Kane is involved.'

'It don't mean he's goin' to Buford,' Rio pointed out.

'You see that feller at the bar with the glasses?'

'Yeah.'

'Well, he's the telegraphist feller in town here,' Utah said excitedly. 'And he said that a wire come for Cassidy and it was sent by Jordan Kane.'

Rio remained silent as he digested the information.

'But that ain't all, Rio,' Utah explained. 'Guess who else is down there?'

'Lucas Kane,' Rio answered, deflating the young Utah.

Rio sat the shot glass on the table top and stood up. He turned away and began to weave his way through the crowded saloon.

Utah jumped up to follow him.

'Where you goin', Rio?' he called after him.

'Buford.'

'What for?'

'To help a friend.'

Utah hurried after him. 'Damn it, wait for me. I ain't missin' out on this.'

CHAPTER 11

'There's someone here to see you, Kane,' Hughes announced.

Lucas Kane looked up from where he was washing in the clear waters of Cottonwood Creek. The large cottonwood trees branched out over the water course and their leaves let through a filtered light.

Walking towards him with Hughes was Brock Hamilton.

'What's up?' asked Kane.

'Hamilton here has some news about some new arrivals in town,' Hughes explained. 'Seems our fears were right. It's been too quiet for too long and now Hamilton here has proof why.'

The gunfighter stood up and stretched out the kinks from where he'd been crouched over the edge of the creek.

He indicated a fallen log and said to the two men, 'Take a seat and fill me in.'

Both men sat down on the rough barked seat and Kane sat on a rock at the water's edge.

'As Ernest said, there's been some new arrivals in town. The last one rode in the day before yesterday,' Hamilton explained. 'Everyone in town has been talkin' about it. That and your brother puttin' pressure on the storekeepers not to sell anythin' to the homesteaders.'

'Who are they?' Kane asked him. 'Did anyone mention names?'

Hamilton thought for a moment as he tried to remember. Then they came to him. 'A big feller someone mentioned, goes by the name of Cassidy. Do you know him?'

Kane nodded grimly. 'Yeah. He's good. Who else?'

'There were four of them,' Hamilton told Kane. 'Johnny Marsh, Roscoe James were two more, the other one that I heard about was some fancy dresser. I don't know his name.'

'The first one who springs to mind is Marty Collins,' Kane said thoughtfully. 'He's another good gun to have on your side. They're all good. From the sounds of it, Lance is goin' all out to put an end to this once and for all.'

A look of concern crept into Hughes' face. 'So this is it? It's what we expected. A shootin' war?'

'It's been a shootin' war,' Kane announced. 'Now they're gettin' serious about it. This time they've hired actual gunfighters and not some wannabe amateurs.'

111

'What do we do? How do we prepare?' Hughes asked, panic adding an edge to his voice.

'You can't do any more than what you're all doin' now,' the gunfighter explained. 'Just remain vigilant. I told you this would come. That you would need to be prepared. Now that it has, you need to be strong. Lead your people from the front.'

'What about you? You can lead us.'

Kane shook his head. 'I'm just a fighter. You're their leader. They respect you. They need someone to give them faith in what they're doin' and you're it.'

'I hope you are right, Kane,' Hughes mumbled.

'I know I am.'

Kane's gaze drifted across to Hamilton. 'How are you doin' in town?'

'We're managing,' Hamilton allowed. 'Martha is doing some work with Ezra Stone and I'm doing bits here and there. It's not a lot but hopefully, we'll be able to get started on building our new house soon. Although, I'm worried about what will happen if Buford Lance succeeds with his plans.'

'I think it will all be over soon,' Kane speculated. 'I have a feeling that the arrival of those new guns in town is the beginning of the end. We just don't know how it will all play out yet. You'd best get on home, Brock. Thanks for the warnin' about the extra guns. And one more thing, keep your family safe.'

Hamilton nodded. 'I will. But you watch your back.'

Kane smiled mirthlessly. 'Don't worry about me. When my killer comes for me, it won't be from behind.'

Martha Hamilton smiled warmly at her husband and daughter as they entered the doctor's surgery.

'To what do I owe the pleasure of this visit?' she asked.

'We thought that seeing it was after dark, we would escort you back to the boarding house,' her husband explained.

'How sweet,' she beamed and leaned in to kiss her husband on the cheek. Then she whispered, 'Did you warn him?'

Hamilton waited for Martha to draw back then gave her a slight nod. 'Yeah. I did.'

'Did what, Daddy?' Elsie asked.

Hamilton pulled a funny face at her and said in a hoarse voice, 'Never you mind.'

His daughter giggled and instantly forgot the question she'd asked.

'You're funny,' she cried out excitedly.

He scooped her up in his arms and looked at Martha. 'Are you ready?'

'Sure, I'll get my shawl.'

Martha left the room and returned a short time later with her shawl wrapped around her shoulders. 'Now I'm ready, let's go.'

Hamilton put Elsie down and looped his arm so

Martha could slip her arm through his.

'You don't want to let the doc know you're leavin'?' Hamilton asked.

'Ezra is busy so I'll let him be,' Martha told her husband and started dragging him towards the door. 'Come on.'

Outside in the night sky, the silvery half-moon had no effect over the dimly lit streets of Buford. The spaced out kerosene lamps lit the boardwalks sporadically and left the alley mouths shrouded in an all-encompassing darkness.

The streets were pretty much empty which was a common occurrence of late, given the trouble and the death of the town's previous sheriff. There was a slight chill in the air and Martha drew her shawl around her a little tighter.

As they approached the alley between the laundry and the assayer's office, a lone figure emerged and stood at the edge of the shadows. Martha reflexively tightened her grip on her husband's arm.

He sensed her tension and patted her gently on the hand. He said softly, 'It's fine.'

Then two more emerged and stood beside the other figure. When the Hamiltons were close enough, the man in the middle spoke. 'Nice evenin' for a walk.'

Hamilton instantly recognized the voice of Jordan Kane and fear began to course through his body. He hated himself for allowing it to happen but the fear was more for his wife and child than himself.

'What. . . ?' Hamilton cleared his throat. 'What can I do for you, Sheriff?'

'I want your daughter,' Jordan said, devoid of emotion.

'No!' Martha gasped out and shielded Elsie with her body.

'The hell you say,' Hamilton managed to get out in an unsatisfactory act of defiance. 'I'll kill the first man who tries to touch her.'

The sheriff held up a hand. 'Now before you go and do anythin' stupid I'll tell you this. Do as we say and no harm will come to your daughter.'

'No harm will come to her because you ain't goin' to take her,' Hamilton said as he took a step forward.

'Cassidy,' Jordan Kane snapped.

The biggest of the other two men stepped forward and a lightning fist snaked out and slammed into Brock Hamilton's middle. The home-steader bent double as air whooshed from his lungs and he sank to his knees. The blow felt as though a mule had kicked him and he struggled desperately to breathe.

Hamilton heard his wife's frantic scream and Elsie cry out for him. His head snapped up and he could make out the other man lifting a kicking and scream-ing Elsie from her feet and tucking her under his arm as one would a sack of flour.

115

Martha Hamilton lunged at the man in a desperate attempt to stop him from taking her child. The man batted her away with his free hand and she fell to all fours in the mouth of the dark alleyway.

A blinding rage overcame Brock and all sense of fear disappeared. He surged to his feet and his arms reached out for the throat of the man who had his little girl.

Thunder filled the night as flame erupted from the end of Jordan Kane's right-side .45, lighting the alley for a brief instant. The bullet ploughed into Hamilton's chest from the side and knocked him from his feet into a limp pile in the dirt at the edge of the boardwalk.

The last things he heard were his wife's frantic screams and his daughter's cry for help as she disappeared into the dark with her kidnapper.

Martha Hamilton tried to follow them but Jordan Kane and Cassidy blocked her path. As she tried to barge through, Jordan grabbed her arm in a vice-like grip and drew her close. He whispered harshly into her ear.

'Find my brother Lucas,' he ordered her. 'Tell him to come to the minin' shack. He'll know where to go.'

'And what if he won't go?' Martha asked between sobs.

'You better hope he does,' Jordan warned her. 'Or you'll never see your daughter again.'

Martha Hamilton's right hand flew to her mouth at the thought of harm befalling Elsie.

'Please don't hurt her,' she begged.

'I guess that's up to Lucas, ma'am, and how good you are at convincing him.'

Without further word the two men turned and disappeared into the darkness.

A low moan sounded from Brock Hamilton as the pain of his wound roused him back to consciousness.

'Brock!' Martha cried out and rushed to her wounded husband's side.

'Elsie?' Hamilton gasped. 'Where's Elsie?'

Martha swallowed the large lump which had formed in her throat. 'They took her, Brock. They took our little girl.'

CHAPTER 12

Lucas Kane had just poured a steaming-hot cup of black coffee when the shouted warning of a rider approaching filled the mist-shrouded morning.

His hand dropped to his Peacemaker and he stood from his seat beside the fire. The rattle of hastily discarded plates and cups filled the still morning air while on-edge settlers prepared once again for the unexpected. The thunder of hoofs grew louder.

Kane frowned as the rider emerged from the mist. It was a woman, but not just any woman. It was Martha Hamilton. From the looks of her flagging mount, something was seriously wrong.

The gunfighter threw down his cup as a wave of foreboding descended upon him. He walked out to meet her and before the horse had stopped, Kane could see the distraught expression on her face.

Martha Hamilton virtually fell from the saddle

into his arms. She was a sobbing wreck and kept blubbering, 'He's got her. He's got her.'

Kane took her firmly by the shoulders as more settlers gathered around.

'Martha – stop,' he ordered. 'Tell me what's happened.'

She stepped back and looked up at him through tear-filled eyes. Pain was etched all over her face and it took a brief moment for Martha to compose herself enough to speak.

'It's . . . it's Elsie,' she managed. 'He took her and shot Br . . . Brock.'

'Who, Martha?' Kane asked calmly.

Martha Hamilton's expression took on a dramatic change. Her eyes blazed and her face contorted as her built-up rage surfaced.

'Your brother, damn you,' she hissed. 'Jordan shot my husband and took my little girl and it's your fault.'

Martha lashed out and slapped him with an open hand. There was a resounding crack as the blow landed on his cheek.

Kane grabbed both of her arms before any follow-up blows could land.

'Let me go!' she shrieked. 'Damn you!'

Martha struggled against his grip but it was no use. She couldn't break free.

She sank once more into Kane's arms and her body convulsed with a new onslaught of wracking sobs.

A muffled murmur rippled through the gathered crowd at what they'd seen.

The gunfighter gave the distraught woman a minute and when her crying had eased he moved her away from him and said, 'Tell me what happened, Martha. And then I'll go and get your little girl back.'

Martha Hamilton composed herself and started at the beginning and filled Kane in on the previous evening's events. He stopped her when she mentioned the shooting of her husband again.

'Is Brock still alive?'

'Yes,' she nodded. 'He was when I left. The doctor managed to get the bullet out. He said that if Brock survived the next day or so, he would be fine.'

'Why did Jordy take Elsie?'

'They want you to go to the mining shack, wherever that is. He said you would know.'

Kane nodded.

'He also said that if you didn't go, I'd never see Elsie again.'

'You know that this could well be a trap, don't you?' Hughes spoke up. It was what they were all thinking but he was the one to give voice to it.

'It is somethin' I considered,' Kane allowed.

'Then do you think it's wise to go there?'

Martha Hamilton clutched desperately at Kane's arm. 'But you must go. Please. If you don't. . . .'

Her voice trailed away and Kane told her reassuringly, 'I'm going, have no fear. And I'm goin' to get

Elsie back. Now get yourself some rest.'

'I can't, I have to get back to Brock,' she protested.

'Rest first,' Kane said firmly. 'Then somebody will go with you back to town to make sure you're OK.'

He watched as Martha was led away by Rose Hughes toward the Hughes' wagon.

Kane silently cursed Jordy for making it come to this. The situation had reached a point that he'd wanted to avoid by all means possible.

Now his hand was being forced and he knew that one brother was not going to survive the impending storm.

'Take some of us with you.' Hughes' voice interrupted his thoughts.

Kane turned and looked at him. He shook his head and said, 'No. It's more than likely a trap for me, but it could be a ploy to get me out of the way so they can hit here. Either way I'm goin'. I owe that family for savin' my life when I was shot.'

He rubbed absent-mindedly at the wound through his clothes. 'And I'm goin' to do everythin' I can to save that little girl. I'm sorry but you'll be on your own for a while.'

A middle-aged man Kane knew as Puller stepped forward.

'You do what you need to do to get that little girl back to her ma, Kane,' he stated. 'We'll be fine while you're gone.'

Virtually as one, the remaining onlookers voiced

their agreement to what had just been said.

'Make sure you all remain vigilant,' Kane reminded them.

Fifteen minutes later Kane rode out, headed for the shack.

The rider hidden in the trees on the ridge line watched as the woman rode into the homesteaders' camp. He waited while events unfolded and then he watched Kane leave.

After which he turned his horse and headed back towards the B-L connected.

When Roscoe James rode into the ranch yard, Lance and Jordan Kane were waiting for him with ranch foreman, Chuck. He climbed down and strode across the hard-packed yard with purpose.

'Well?' asked Lance impatiently.

'He rode out after he talked to the woman,' James told him.

Lance looked across at his foreman. 'Chuck, you know what to do. You need to keep him there all night without gettin' yourself or any of the others killed.'

'We can manage that,' Chuck assured him.

'Pull out just before the sun comes up,' Lance told him. 'Once he finds out what has happened, I'm more than certain he'll go to town lookin' for his brother. That's where him and the others will be waitin'.'

'What about the girl?' Chuck asked.

'We'll keep her here until it's all done,' Lance told him.

Jordan knew that the ranch foreman had never liked the idea of taking Elsie Hamilton, but he'd held his tongue.

'I'll get gone then,' Chuck said.

After the foreman had walked off, Roscoe James asked Lance, 'Can we trust him to do his job?'

'I've known that man for a long time,' Lance told him. 'He may not agree with what we did to that girl, but he'll do what needs to be done. Rest assured.'

'I hope so. The last thing we need is for Lucas Kane to appear in the middle of a gun fight to rally the homesteaders. At least, without him, they'll have no organisation.'

Kane rode out of the trees and hauled back on the buckskin's reins. He sat there and studied the shack. He immediately knew that something wasn't right.

Firstly there was no smoke coming from the chimney. There were no horses in the corral and he could see no fresh tracks on the ground.

He reached down and drew an 1876 model Winchester from the saddle boot. The '76 was chambered for a .45-.75 calibre cartridge and had enough stopping power to bring down a grizzly. On a man it was devastating.

Kane levered a round into the breech and sat

there for a further five minutes, waiting and watching. When there was still no sign of life, he kneed the buckskin forward and approached the shack at a slow pace.

Hidden away in the trees and rocks to his left were the riders from the B-L connected. Chuck had told them to remain that way until he, and he alone, fired the first shot. They'd been threatened with a beating and being fired if they didn't follow his instructions to the letter. Every man knew that Chuck was as good as his word.

'What are we waitin' for, Chuck?' whispered a wiry cowhand.

'We're waitin' for him to go inside,' Chuck whispered harshly. 'Now shut up.'

There were five of them in all. Cowhands, not gunmen, but they rode for the brand and every now and then they would draw fighting wages, such as they were now.

They waited and watched as Kane moved closer to the mining shack.

As Kane drew nearer the shack, he became absolutely certain that there was nobody here. It put him on edge. He scanned the tree line and was almost certain that he caught a glimpse of red clothing hidden away amongst the rocks to his left.

He made the decision to ride on. He was closer to

the shack than the trees so it would be pointless to turn back now.

He braced himself for the inevitable but nothing happened. He drew up in front of the shack but still the day remained peaceful.

Once he'd dismounted, Kane kept the buckskin between himself and the tree line. He used it until he reached the doorway then slapped it hard on the rump.

'Heeyaah!' Kane shouted and the animal leaped forward and bolted away from where he stood.

With all his strength he hit the door with his shoulder. It flew wide and he disappeared inside.

As he suspected it was empty. Now he had a problem. He was trapped.

Kane edged his way over to the window and peered out. He studied the tree line and as he inadvertently moved out to get a better look, a rifle shot rang out.

The bullet hit a thin plank near the window which sounded like a hammer driving a nail into it. The slug punched through and sent splinters that flew dangerously around the small room.

Kane ducked back and cursed himself for being a fool. He was trapped with no idea how many men were out there. At least one that he knew of but he was certain there were more.

He peered out the window more cautiously this time. Whoever was out there was well hidden. He ducked into a crouch and moved to the window on the other side of the front door.

As he passed the open door, rifle fire opened up again. This time with three more shots.

All bored holes in the front wall up high. Kane dropped flat as two more shots rang out. These last ones came from a different rifle and the window he was headed for shattered, spraying glass everywhere.

The gunfighter tentatively rose to his feet and looked around the corner of the window frame and out through the now glassless window. At the edge of the tree line, Kane could make out the faint wisp of gunsmoke, giving away the position of at least one shooter.

The barrel of the Winchester '76 slid over the sill and Kane thumbed back the hammer. He fired three times. Evenly spaced shots to see what kind of reaction he would get.

The response was immediate and the rifles in the tree line erupted in a violent fusillade of shots. This time, the gunfighter didn't duck down. There was no need to. Once more, all shots went high.

'Looks as though they want to keep me here but not kill me,' Kane pondered.

He knew that would be Jordan's doing. It also meant that his brother was not there or they would have come face to face by now.

Why lure him out here if they were going to ambush him and not kill him? The answer was simple. They wanted him out of the way to get at the homesteaders. A ploy, he guessed. Take the girl, send him on a wild goose chase and hit the settlers while he was out of the way.

And it had worked well. He was stuck in the shack with no way out.

The sun sank behind the high mountains and took all its warmth with it. The evening air was left with a cool chill. Kane had worked out that there were five men out there. He'd hit one for sure. The screams of the wounded man had echoed around the surrounding high country for at least a half hour before they'd died away. So he was either unconscious or dead.

Outside the shack, the remnants of daylight had turned the cold, pale grey colour of dusk that provided a muted illumination of the landscape just before full dark. The gunfire had ceased some time ago, but the men were still out there.

Kane found some tins of beans in a cupboard and used an old knife to open them, then ate them cold.

There was a lantern and firewood but he wasn't about to use them because he wasn't planning on being there long enough.

While he'd been waiting for dark, Kane had worked off some planks at the back of the shack. After it was completely dark he was going to venture out and take care of whoever was out there.

'At least Clem is quiet now,' the wiry cowhand said sounding relieved. 'All that wailin' was getting' on my nerves.'

'That's because he's dead, you dumb ass,' Chuck whispered harshly. 'Now, shut up and keep an eye out just in case Kane sneaks out of there.'

'He ain't goin' nowhere and he knows it,' the cowboy declared. 'That's why he ain't bothered to shoot no more.'

Chuck ignored him. He wished he had his confidence but something told him that Kane wasn't most men and by now he'd worked out the whys and wherefores of what was going on. And he would not take it lying down.

Somewhere in the darkness, a dry twig snapped. Chuck tensed and dropped his hand to the butt of his six-gun. He held his breath and waited.

'Who's there?' a cowboy's frightened voice asked. 'Answer me.'

Suddenly the night was filled with the roar of guns and the flicker of muzzle-flashes. Chuck heard a man cry out in pain and felt hot air scorch his neck at the passing of a bullet.

Another cowboy screamed as he was shot in the belly, the bullet from the Winchester that Kane was using blew a huge hole in his back as it exited.

Chuck drew his six-gun and began to fire blindly.

He fired two shots and heard a shout when one of his bullets found its mark.

The sound of gunfire died away and darkness enveloped Chuck once more. The only thing he could hear was the dry rasp of his own heavy breathing.

'Doug, Hank, Willie, are you there?' Chuck called warily. 'Doug, Willie, answer me. Did you get him?'

'They're all dead,' came Kane's voice from the darkness. 'You killed the last one.'

'Damn you,' Chuck cursed and squeezed the trigger on his six-gun.

The roar of the shot filled the night and the orange flame that spouted from the gun's barrel illuminated the darkness.

The echoes died away and Kane's voice spoke calmly. 'Where's my brother?'

Chuck's gaze flicked left and right as he tried to pin-point the exact location of the voice.

'He's gone after the settlers with the others.'

'Where's the girl?' Kane asked.

'Where you sure as hell can't get her,' Chuck snarled and fired once more, missing his intended target in the confusion of the dark.

This time, Kane fired back and the .45-.75 slug punched into Chuck's chest, tunnelled through and destroyed everything in its path then exploded out his back in an unseen spray of blood.

The B-L connected foreman grunted in surprise

and collapsed into a heap on the damp earth at his feet.

Out of the blackness came Kane's voice one final time. 'I wouldn't be so sure of that.'

CHAPTER 13

Roscoe James emerged from the curtain of darkness, wiping the blade of his knife on his sleeve.

The moon was up now which cast a dull silvery glow over Cottonwood Creek and the homesteaders' camp below.

'Damn fool sodbuster was asleep,' James snorted. 'I could've blown a damn bugle and he still wouldn't have heard me comin'.'

'Mount up and let's earn our money,' Jordan Kane said.

The five men drew their guns and moved their mounts out of the trees to start down the slope of the hill. Below them, all appeared quiet, but it wouldn't be for long.

If it had been daylight, things would have been quite different. At night, however, even with the moon up and at this pace, the trail was treacherous. A couple of times the buckskin had stumbled and almost fallen, but the animal had managed to gather itself and kept going.

Kane urged it on but knew full well that he would be too late to stop what was planned.

A deep rumble brought Hughes awake. His first thought was a storm but he realized that the noise he judged to be thunder was constant.

He frowned. Still half-asleep, it took a little longer for his foggy mind to process what his ears could hear.

By then it was too late.

The night was rent with the sound of gunfire. It was closely followed by cries of alarm, screams of women and children and the sound of dying.

Hughes rolled out of his bedroll and scooped up his rifle. On the far side of the camp muzzle flashes lit the night as gunfire rang out in its staccato rhythm.

'Ernest! What's happening?' Rose Hughes' fearful cry reached her husband's ears through the din.

'Get under the wagon and stay there,' he called back. 'Don't come out.'

The gunfire grew closer and horses thundered by him, so he was forced to dive on to the damp grass and out of the way. Behind him he heard the muffled scream of a settler as the charge mowed them down.

Hughes climbed to a knee and lifted the rifle. He sighted down the barrel and squeezed the trigger.

The gun slammed back against his shoulder and flame spewed from its muzzle.

He cursed as his shot flew wide and fired a second for the same result as the riders disappeared into the night beyond the camp firelight. Hughes could hear the riders yelling to each other and realized they were turning around for another run.

Once more the riders stormed out of the darkness with the advantage of the settler's campfire illuminating targets. Their guns erupted and a new storm of lead filled the air.

Hughes felt a slug tear at his jacket and another cracked loudly as it passed close to his head. Instinctively Hughes ducked then regained some composure and jacked another round into the breach of the Winchester.

He swung the rifle up at the oncoming riders and fired in their direction, levered in a new round and fired again.

An anguished cry came from one of the riders who leaned sideways in the saddle. The wounded rider straightened up and kept on riding.

He surprised Hughes by angling his mount towards him. A straight line course that would bring him into direct contact with the settler.

Hughes frantically worked the lever of the rifle and fired as fast as he could. All of the shots went wide and then the hammer fell upon the empty chamber.

Fear filled Hughes as the rider thundered towards him. The killer's gun sounded twice and Hughes felt the impact as both bullets struck him.

The homesteader dropped the rifle as all of his strength ebbed. He sank slowly to his knees as the rider galloped past him, close enough to reach out and touch.

Hughes struggled to breathe as his lungs started to fill with blood. He could feel it welling up in his throat. He coughed and tried to clear it so he could draw another breath.

Somewhere he heard Rose calling his name. *I just need a minute, Rose,* he thought *and then I'll be there.*

Exhaustion enveloped him and his eyes started to close. *Just a little nap, Rose and then I'll be fine.*

Hughes felt no pain, just an all-pervading numbness. His breaths grew shallower and shallower then he canted to the right until he lay on the churned-up grass.

A couple more shallow gasps were all he could manage, though he was oblivious to the death that surrounded him.

Kane crested the hill on the foam-flecked buckskin and hauled back on the reins. The scene that greeted him from below was one of utter devastation. Burned-out wagons, bodies laid out in a row and settlers milling about, totally numb from the shocking attack of the previous night.

Kane cursed under his breath and steeled himself for what was to come before he rode down from the hill. He knew it was bad, he could see as much from his position. He just hoped it wasn't as bad as he feared.

He kneed the buckskin forward at a slow walk. Several of the homesteaders turned and saw his approach but showed no reaction to his presence.

Puller emerged from a group near a burnt-out wagon. He met Kane at the edge of the camp. Pain was etched all over the man's face.

'How many?' Kane asked solemnly.

'Ten,' Puller said in a low voice. 'The girl?'

Kane shook his head. 'She wasn't there. They just wanted to get me out of the way. They bottled me up in the shack. I tried to get back here as fast as I could.'

'It ain't your fault,' Puller told him.

Kane looked about then asked Puller, 'Hughes?'

The homesteader moved his head in the general direction and said, 'Over there.'

Kane glanced across to where Puller had indicated and saw only bodies. He looked back and gave him a questioning look.

The man nodded.

Kane dropped his gaze for a moment then climbed down from his horse. He walked across to the line of bodies and saw the man he looked for.

Laid out between an elderly man and his own wife,

was Ernest Hughes. He looked pale and peaceful, his front covered with dried brown blood. Rose Hughes looked just as peaceful, even with the dark hole in the centre of her forehead.

Kane turned away, his teeth clenched and his jaw set firm. It was all he could do to keep his deep rage in check.

He looked at Puller and asked, 'How many were there?'

'Five,' the homesteader answered. 'I think Ernest might have winged one before he was killed. His wife was found under their wagon.'

Kane turned to walk away and Puller stopped him.

'Where are you goin'?' he asked.

'I'm goin' to town.'

'On your own?' Puller questioned. 'If you wait until we bury our dead some of us will come with you.'

Kane shook his head.

'No,' he said with finality. 'This is what I do. Besides, you people have already lost enough.'

Pent up anger flared in Puller. 'They were our people, damn it.'

'And he's my brother,' Kane snapped. 'He wanted a showdown and now he's goin' to get it. It should've happened before now but I thought I could avoid it. All it achieved was the deaths of so many innocent people and a little girl kidnapped. And by hell it's goin' to stop.'

Puller went to add more but remained quiet when he saw the cold look in the gunfighter's eyes.

'If I get killed, leave,' Kane ordered.

The homesteader's eyes grew wide. 'What? After all we've been through you're tellin' us to give up? People fought and died for this land and there is no way in hell that they'll leave.'

'If you don't go, they'll bury the rest of you here,' Kane told him bluntly. 'Go and come back with some real law. If you don't, more of you will die.'

The gunfighter didn't wait for Puller to speak. He turned on his heel and strode off towards his played-out mount.

'Kane!' Puller called after him.

Kane turned around.

'At least, let me get you a fresh horse.'

'That would be good,' Kane allowed. 'Thanks.'

Ten minutes later the gunfighter left the devastation of the homesteaders' camp astride a big chestnut horse that Puller had given him.

CHAPTER 14

Kane eased the powerful animal down to a walk as he hit the outskirts of Buford. Once the horse had slowed enough, he pointed it towards a solid-looking hitch-rail outside Sigurd's blacksmith shop.

Sigurd emerged while Kane was tying the horse to the rail. He was a big man with blond hair. The sleeves on his shirt had been torn off exposing large muscles in his arms.

He looked at Kane. 'You are here for them, *ja*?'

Kane nodded. 'Yeah.'

The big man shook his head solemnly. 'It is a bad thing they did. It is not right for them to do this.'

'Where are they?' the gunfighter asked as he took the Winchester from the saddle boot.

Sigurd looked surprised. 'You do this alone?'

'Yeah,' Kane said patiently. 'Where are they?'

The big man shrugged. 'Maybe the jail.'

He pulled out a six-gun he had tucked in his belt.

The size of it compared to his hand seemed awfully small.

'I help,' he said taking a step forward.

'No.'

'But there are five of them.'

'So folks keep sayin'.'

Kane walked off and left Sigurd standing there scratching his head.

It was a slow walk along the main street of Buford. The sun was high in the sky and threw short shadows. Townsfolk watched cautiously as he passed then they quickly disappeared from sight. They knew what was coming. Word had spread like wild-fire about the previous night's happenings on the Cottonwood Creek range.

Kane's eyes darted left and right taking everything in. His right hand rested on the butt of the Peacemaker, the hammer thong had been flipped off earlier. In his left hand, Kane held the Winchester, leant back on his shoulder.

A fully laden freight wagon trundled along the street drawn by two mules, so he was forced to walk further to the left while it passed. A lone rider took one look at Kane then turned his horse around and rode in the opposite direction.

Kane spotted two women who stood talking on the boardwalk outside of the drapery. Both turned in his direction and he recognized Martha Hamilton straight away. The other woman he had never seen before.

Martha Hamilton ended the conversation abruptly, stepped down from the boardwalk and hurried across to the gunfighter.

'What happened?' she asked worriedly. 'Where's Elsie?'

'I'm sorry, Martha,' Kane apologized. 'She wasn't there.'

Tears welled in her eyes and her bottom lip began to tremble.

'Well, where is she, damn it?' she flared.

'I don't know,' he explained softly. 'But as soon as I find out I'll tell you.'

Through tear-filled eyes she stared at him then her expression changed when she realized what he was about to do.

'Oh God. You're going down there to face them, aren't you?'

'It has to be done.'

'But he's your brother,' Martha reminded him, placing a slender-fingered hand on his arm.

'Jordan ceased to be my brother when he and that bunch of his killed Ernest Hughes and his wife last night, along with eight others,' Kane said flatly.

'But what about Elsie?'

'She's just a pawn in the whole scheme of things,' Kane assured her. 'They won't hurt her. They got what they wanted.'

Kane stepped around her and continued his walk towards what some would see as fate.

Ahead of him, word had spread and the street was empty. The bat-wing doors of the Nugget saloon swung open with a high-pitched squeak which caused Kane to turn in that direction. His Peacemaker was halfway out of its holster before he stopped himself.

'Gettin' a might jumpy of late, Lucas,' Rio Smith said as he stepped down off the boardwalk into the street.

'What in hell are you doin' here?' Kane asked.

'We thought you might be needin' some help,' Rio explained.

'We?'

A young man stepped out into clear view from behind Rio.

'More him than me,' the young man said enthusiastically. 'But I sure wasn't goin' to miss this.'

Kane raised his eyebrows at Rio.

'He's a might over eager but he's fast,' Rio told him. 'I heard Jordan was in town?'

'You heard right,' Kane nodded. And then, 'What's his name?'

'Calls himself Utah,' Rio told him. 'Word is that Jordan's got four other guns with him.'

'Uh-huh.'

'If I haven't missed my guess, I'd say you're on your way to see him now.'

Kane nodded. 'Has he been readin' too many dime novels?'

Rio looked puzzled. 'Who? Jordan?'

'No. The kid.' Kane stared hard at Utah. 'What's your name, kid?'

The young man opened his mouth, thought about answering then snapped it shut. He thought some more and said, 'Byron.'

'I can see why you like Utah,' Kane sighed. 'And you want in on this?'

'Rio rode a hundred miles to deal himself in,' Utah explained. 'That's good enough for me.'

'Who're we up against?' Rio asked.

'Jordy, Johnny Marsh, Roscoe James, Marty Collins and Cassidy.'

Rio whistled, then drew his Colt as was his habit before all gunfights and checked the loads. He snapped the loading gate shut and holstered it.

'Let's go and pay them boys a visit, huh?'

Kane looked at the Winchester in his left hand. He walked across to the boardwalk and leaned it against a veranda post. He walked back out into the street and said, 'Yeah, let's.'

All five gunmen were lounging out the front of the jail and when Jordan Kane saw the three men walking side-by-side along the street towards them, he smiled.

'Looks like Lucas has got himself some help,' he said with an air of expectation.

Cassidy spat on the boardwalk. 'Hell, it's Rio and the kid, Utah.'

'A no-name and a kid,' Jordan sneered. 'Lucas must be scrapin' the bottom of the barrel.'

'Don't underestimate them, Jordan,' Cassidy cautioned. 'You may not have seen them in action but I have. Rio is good. Real good. He just don't go lookin' for a name for hisself. And Utah, he may be young but he's as fast as they come.'

'They're your problem, not mine,' Jordan said dismissively. 'The only one I have to worry about is Lucas. I kill him, and I take his place at the top of the tree.'

For the first time, Cassidy saw a wild, almost crazed look in the younger Kane's eyes. He knew then that it was all going to end badly.

Too late to back out now, he reasoned. Things had gone too far. They'd seen to that the previous night when they'd slaughtered the settlers.

'Come on,' Jordan said as he stood and stepped down into the street.

The others followed him and fanned out, three feet between each man. Jordan Kane stood at the end of the line where he could man up to his brother.

'Do you feel it, Cassidy?' he asked the big gunman.

'Feel what?'

Jordan looked across at Cassidy with the same wild look as before. 'The feelin' you get right before the battle. The feelin' of invincibility.'

'You crazy son of a bitch,' Cassidy mumbled and shook his head.

Kane watched as the five gunmen ahead of him fanned out across the street. As they stood from left to right they were Collins, Cassidy, James, Marsh, and Jordan. Collins looked to be holding himself stiffly. He would be the wounded one, Kane guessed.

The trio closed the distance between them at a steady pace.

'What do you think?' Rio asked Kane.

'I think if we get out of this with our hides intact we'll be three of the luckiest sons of bitches around,' the gunfighter said drily.

The gap had closed to sixty feet. The five killers had stopped, allowing the others to approach.

'How you feelin', kid?' Kane asked Utah.

'I'll tell you when this is over,' he answered nervously.

'You can still back out,' Rio informed him. 'No one would think any less of you.'

'I would,' Utah said.

Fifty feet.

'Utah,' Kane said without taking his eyes from the men in front of him. 'As soon as it starts, don't stand still. Just keep movin' and shootin'.'

'Why?'

'Because you'll stay alive a lot longer that way,' Rio elaborated.

All remained quiet until the two groups were thirty

feet apart. Kane decided that was close enough and stopped.

Jordan smiled. 'So the time has come, huh, brother?'

'You shouldn't have killed all them settlers, Jordy,' Kane said.

'That was the job, Lucas.'

'No, Jordy. That was just plain murder,' Kane told him. 'The act of a mad dog killer.'

Kane glanced along the line of men. All were on edge. Gunhands tightened on gun butts, poised to pull in the blink of an eye.

His eyes came back to Jordan.

His brother smiled coldly and moved his feet a little wider. 'You plan on doin' somethin' about it?'

'Someone has to,' Kane allowed.

Then something strange happened. Something that, in the eyes of Jordan Kane, wasn't right.

Casually Kane moved to his left behind Rio who in turn had moved to his right.

'What the hell is this?' Jordan snapped. 'Get the hell back here.'

'When you're ready, Jordy,' Kane said flatly. 'Get the ball started.'

The younger Kane was confused. 'No. This ain't the way it's supposed to be. It's me and you. I ain't pullin' on him.'

'You'd better, kid,' Rio told him. 'I'm goin' to pull on you.'

'The hell you are!' Jordan shrieked and spittle flew from his lips. 'This is not how it's meant to be! It is me and Lucas! And when I kill him I will be the new king!'

Kane saw the wild look in his brother's eyes and almost felt sorry for him. But it reinforced what Jordan Kane really was; a crazed killer.

'The hell with this.'

Kane's eyes snapped across to Cassidy who had turned away and started to walk off.

'Where are you going, Cassidy?' Jordan shouted.

'I'm through with you, Jordan,' the big gunfighter said without turning. 'You're outta your head. I must've been stupid to get mixed up with you in the first place.'

'Stop,' Jordan called after him.

'Go to hell.'

'I said stop, you coward!'

As Jordan's shriek filled the street he drew his right side Colt and shot Cassidy in the back. The roar of the shot reverberated from the false-front shops that lined the street. The big gunman fell face down from the hammer blow impact of the slug.

No one heard the second shot. The thunder of the first had drowned it out.

Jordan Kane turned and looked at his brother then at the smoking Peacemaker he held in his hand. He pressed his left hand to his side, just up from his bottom rib. He looked bemused at his hand as it came away dripping with bright-red blood.

The others noticed the dark stain gradually build in size on his clothing as his life flowed from the hole the bullet had made.

Jordan gave Kane a wan smile and managed to say, 'I knew you couldn't beat me, Lucas. You had to wait until I wasn't looking.'

Slowly, like some giant tree being felled in the forest, Jordan Kane hit the dirt of Buford's main street and didn't move. The killer they called the Prince was dead.

'Don't even think about it,' Rio hissed.

Kane's gaze snapped away from his dead brother and he saw that both Rio and Utah had their guns drawn and had the remaining hired guns covered.

'Unbuckle 'em slow and easy,' Rio ordered.

The three gunmen did as they were told and let their gunbelts drop at their feet.

'What are you doin', Rio?' Roscoe James asked.

'You're goin' to jail,' Rio informed him. 'Where I suspect you will remain until they hang you all.'

'The hell I am,' James blurted out.

Utah thumbed back the hammer on his six-gun. 'Can I shoot him, Rio?'

'Wait,' Kane said stepping forward. 'Before you do, where's the girl?'

'Let us go and I'll tell you,' James offered.

Kane drew his Peacemaker and closed the distance between himself and the killer. He placed the cold, hard gun barrel against James' head and whispered harshly, 'I just killed my own brother. I'm in no mood to be bandyin' words with a piece of trash like you. Where is the girl?'

Beads of sweat broke out on James' forehead and he trembled slightly. Still, there was no information forthcoming. The hired killer closed his eyes; his jaw remained clenched shut as though he was bracing himself for the death blow.

The dry triple-click of the gun hammer going back on the Peacemaker changed all of that.

'The girl?'

'Wait,' James bleated, 'I'll tell you. Lance has her, out at his ranch.'

Kane let down the hammer and holstered the Colt.

'Now you can lock 'em up,' he told Rio.

'Are you goin' after the girl?'

'Yeah.'

'Want some help?'

'No. I can handle it.'

'Fair enough.'

CHAPTER 15

The big chestnut crossed the stream and climbed the small cut with powerful strides. When it topped the bank Kane urged it on and the animal thundered into the B-L connected ranch yard.

Two cowboys breaking a horse in the corral scooped up rifles and hurried towards the gunfighter.

Kane was out of the saddle in the blink of an eye and strode purposefully towards the house when they stopped in front of him.

'Can we help you, mister?' they asked.

'I've come to see your boss,' he told them.

'Mr Lance said that he don't want no visitors today,' the thin cowboy on the left said.

'Paid us a five-dollar bonus to see he weren't disturbed,' the thick-set cowboy on the right put in.

Kane stepped forward, angling for the gap between the two men.

'He'll see me.'

The cowboys blocked his way. 'Nope. Don't think he will.'

Kane took a step back and looked at both men. The look of determination on both of their faces told him the pair weren't going to budge. After all, five dollars for a cowboy was almost a week's wage.

'Listen very carefully, both of you,' Kane started. 'In that house behind you, your boss is holdin' a little girl hostage. I'm here to get her.'

'The boss said no one,' the thin cowboy said.

Kane sighed resignedly. Then with a blur of movement too fast for the eye to see, he drew his Peacemaker and shot both of them.

The two cowboys went down screaming, clutching at their wounded legs. Kane stepped forward and kicked their rifles away from them.

'Count yourselves lucky you ain't dead,' he told them. 'If there hadn't been so much killin' lately I just might have put them slugs in both your heads.'

The gunfighter opened the loading gate on the Peacemaker and dropped out the two empties. He took two from the loops of his gunbelt and replaced the ones he'd taken out.

After which he headed for the ranch house.

As soon as Kane opened one side of the twin front doors, the deep throaty roar of a shotgun greeted him. Wooden splinters were gouged from the door to his left as the charge of buckshot ploughed into it.

They scythed dangerously through the air and a sliver scored the gunfighter's neck. The small cut burned and Kane rubbed at it with the back of his hand. When he took it away, there was blood on it.

Kane cursed himself for not being careful enough. His only thought had been for the girl and just busting into the house had almost gotten him killed.

'Give it up, Lance,' Kane called out. 'It's all over.'

'Go to hell, Kane,' the rancher shouted back.

'Come on, Lance, it's finished. They're all dead or in jail.'

'Chuck? Did you shoot him?'

'Yeah.'

A loud curse was followed by the discharge of the second barrel of the shotgun. This time, the door took the brunt of it and a fist-sized chunk was torn away.

Kane looked around the corner of the doorway and saw Lance climbing the stairs. He fired twice at the rancher and his bullets gouged plaster from the walls. He aimed to fire once more but Lance had made it to the landing and disappeared.

Kane edged through the door and crossed warily to the stairs. No sooner had he placed a foot on the bottom step when Lance reappeared. He'd discarded the shotgun and was now armed with a pistol.

He fired twice, both slugs burned through the air close to Kane's head and ricocheted off the marble floor behind him, hammering into the wood panelling of the wall.

Kane snapped off two more shots but they passed through empty space and smacked into the wall because Lance had disappeared once again.

The gunfighter climbed the stairs and once on the landing, took shelter against the wall at the edge of a long hallway.

He peered around the corner and found the hallway empty. Along each side were two rooms. The doors on all four were open.

Kane ducked back and emptied the Peacemaker's cylinder of the four empty cartridges. He replaced them with fresh rounds and snapped the loading gate shut.

With that done, Kane stayed put and listened. At first, all he could hear was the sound of his own heavy breathing but then he heard a soft whimper drift down the hallway from one of the rooms. It could only be Elsie Hamilton.

Kane stepped out into the hall and on to a board that telegraphed his presence with a loud creak. Alarm ran through him and he dropped to his right knee.

Lance appeared from the second doorway on the left and wildly fired his six-gun three times. Two of the slugs went high and after trying to correct his aim, Lance's third one tore through Kane's jacket and scored a red furrow along his left shoulder.

It threw the gunfighter's aim and the shot he fired missed but the bullet sprayed Lance's face with splinters.

The rancher reeled back into the room and disappeared from sight.

Kane lurched to his feet trying to ignore the dull burning sensation in his shoulder. He moved swiftly along the hall and stopped just outside the room. From inside he could hear the soft, scared cries of Elsie Hamilton. Then Lance's voice whispered harshly, 'Shut up, damn it.'

'Let the girl go, Lance,' Kane called out.

'Now why would I do that and lose the only thing I have to bargain with?'

'Because if you don't I'll come in there and kill you.'

'I don't think so, Kane,' Lance sounded confident. 'You see, I have her in front of me and my six-gun is pointed right at her pretty little head. You do anythin' silly and she's apt to get hurt.'

'What do you want, Lance?' Kane asked him.

'What I want is for you to get on your horse and get the hell outta here.'

'And let you get away with killin' all of those innocent people?'

'They're on my land, damn you!' Lance snarled.

'It's their land, Lance,' Kane reminded him. 'It never was yours.'

'It's always been mine!' Lance shouted. 'I fought

for it and they have no right to be there!'

'I tell you what, Lance, let Elsie go and I'll let you ride out.'

'I already told you how it's goin' to be,' the rancher said calmly. 'I'll give you to the count of three to hear your boots goin' back along the hall. If I don't, then it's all over for the kid.'

Kane heard Elsie's muffled cry and deduced that Lance had his hand over her mouth.

'One!' Lance shouted.

Kane looked down at the Peacemaker in his fist and drew in a deep breath. He closed his eyes then let it out slowly until he felt his entire body relax.

'Two!'

Kane's eyes snapped open and he moved swiftly. His frame filled the doorway and his six-gun was levelled at Lance. It thundered loudly in the confines of the room and the rancher's head snapped back as the .45 slug smashed through his skull.

The unfired pistol dropped from Lance's lifeless hand and thudded on to the carpeted floor. He fell backward and knocked over a small table which stood beside an iron-framed single bed.

'Three,' Kane finished as he stared at the dead man.

Elsie Hamilton screamed loudly and dropped to her knees, sobbing. Kane holstered his gun and rushed forward. He knelt down in front of her and wrapped his arms around her trembling form.

'It's OK,' Kane soothed. 'It's all over now.'

He scooped her up and carried her out the door. Then along the hall and downstairs to the shattered doors.

He sat Elsie on the horse and climbed up behind her. Then he pointed the chestnut towards the grandiose arch he'd ridden through the very first time he'd come to the B-L connected. They passed under it and headed back to town.

CHAPTER 16

When the door to the doctor's recovery room opened, the last person Martha Hamilton expected to see walk in was Kane. The surprise showed on her face and her mouth opened and closed as she tried to make words come out.

'Dang, if it ain't the first time I ever saw her lost for words,' Brock Hamilton said dryly from where he lay in the bed.

'Elsie?' Martha finally said.

Kane smiled and stepped aside as the Hamilton's little girl burst in and threw herself into her mother's arms.

'Oh my lord,' Martha gasped, her eyes filled with tears of joy and relief. 'You've brought our baby back to us.'

Brock looked at Kane, emotion clear in his face as well. 'I don't know what to say. Thank you.'

'Yes, thank you,' joined in Martha. Then she asked, 'Is it over?'

Kane nodded. 'You can go home whenever you like.'

'What about Lance?' Brock asked.

'You don't have to worry about him anymore,' Kane informed them.

'I'm sorry you had . . .' Martha paused. 'You know, about your brother.'

Kane nodded. 'What do you plan on doing now?'

'I don't know,' Kane shrugged. 'Another job maybe. Another town.'

'Why don't you hang around Buford for a while?' Hamilton suggested. 'I'm sure that the town could use a man with your skills. After all, we're goin' to be needin' a sheriff here now.'

Kane opened his mouth to rebuke the suggestion when there was a knock at the door. It swung open and in walked Rio and Utah.

'They said you were back,' Rio explained. 'Hope you don't mind the intrusion, ma'am?'

Martha shook her head. 'No. It's fine, really. Are you the two men who helped Lucas earlier?'

'Yes, ma'am.'

'Then we are grateful to you too. I'm sure that without your help we would never have our Elsie back.'

'We didn't do much, ma'am,' Rio said. 'We just sort of stood there and looked scary.'

'We were just tellin' Kane how much the town needs a sheriff now,' Hamilton explained.

A big smile split Rio's face. 'Were you now?'

'What're you smilin' at?' Kane snapped.

Rio winked at the Hamiltons. 'Oh, nothin'. Although I must admit it sounds a lot better than ridin' herd on a bunch of cows.'

Kane gave him an indignant look. 'I told you the last time we met that I happen to like cows.'

'So I recall.'

Six months later

Kane eased his buckskin to a stop on top of the hill and looked out across the Cottonwood Creek range. A lot had happened since what was now referred to as the 'Homesteader War'.

The homesteaders were finally able to build homes for themselves without fear of being ambushed by raiders. Most of them now had houses and barns built and were able to obtain all the supplies that they needed from town.

The three remaining gunmen were tried and convicted of murder. All of them were hung for their crimes.

Perhaps one of the biggest changes was the town itself. After a meeting, the town committee voted unanimously to change the town's name from Buford to New Hope in an effort to erase the past.

The other big change was Buford Lance's once-great B-L connected ranch. It had been broken up, ironically for quarter sections and the first wagon train of settlers were due in the following week.

The Hamiltons were offered the B-L connected ranch house but they declined the offer. Instead, they rebuilt with the help of the homesteaders and the town.

A noise behind Kane interrupted his thoughts and he hipped in the saddle to see who was approaching.

Riding up the back side of the slope was Utah. The young man drew his horse up beside Kane and asked, 'Where are they?'

'About a mile further on,' Kane explained. 'They're hidden up a gulch. Where's the sheriff?'

'Rio happens to be a little busy at this time,' Utah explained. 'His words not mine. So he sent his deputy to handle this affair.'

'Lisa?' asked Kane.

Utah nodded. 'Yeah, Lisa. Somehow I figure it ain't just her cookin' he's interested in.'

Kane smiled. 'You could be right.'

Utah looked at Kane's hip where the Peace-maker once sat. Now he wore nothing. The six-gun hung on a peg in his small shack built on his own quarter section, a reminder of the life he once lived.

'I thought you might be carryin',' Utah observed.

'I got my Winchester. Besides, I got the law with me. What could possibly go wrong?'

'Yeah, what?' Utah said sceptically. 'Anyway, let's go and find these rustlers that have your cows.'

'Yeah, let's do that.'